"How much do you want?"

Erin's eyes widened. The man who was her husband sat in the driver's seat and repeated dispassionately, "It *is* money you want, isn't it? My problem is fairly well-known. And every now and then someone comes along with a story to fill the gap. Usually there's a child involved and I'm supposed to be the father. Is that your line, or have you come up with something more original?"

Tears blinded her. "No, it's—I...oh, Kirk, I'm your wife! Don't you remember me at all?"

He stared at her without a flicker of recognition. "No, I don't," he said finally, "and if you try this tale again you might find yourself in jail on a charge of fraud!"

Remember Me, My Love

Valerie Parv

Harlequin Books

TORONTO • NEW YORK • LONDON
AMSTERDAM • PARIS • SYDNEY • HAMBURG
STOCKHOLM • ATHENS • TOKYO • MILAN

Original hardcover edition published in 1983
by Mills & Boon Limited

ISBN 0-373-02628-5

Harlequin Romance first edition June 1984

CHAPTER ONE

THE muscles in Erin Wilding's shoulders protested furiously as she lifted another sheet of blue metal from the conveyor belt and thrust it into the stamping machine. She braced herself for the tumult of noise which followed as the machine cut and shaped the metal. Unconsciously, her slender body trembled in time to the throbbing of the giant press.

Every few minutes, her gaze flickered towards the closed door that separated the factory from the executive offices. How she longed to fling herself through that door, run up the steps she knew lay beyond it and walk straight into Don Sands' office to confront him.

But what if she was wrong? What if this was merely another in the series of heartbreaking false leads she had followed during the last three years? No, she would have to force herself to wait until he decided to tour the factory floor, as the other women on the assembly line had assured her he did regularly. Only when she could take a close look at him could she be sure if he was really her husband, Kirk Wilding, who had vanished from the face of the earth nearly three years ago.

In all that time, she had never wavered in her belief that he was still alive. Even when the authorities had come to her door to tell her that Kirk's plane had ditched into the sea and he was presumed drowned, she had refused to accept it. They thought she was suffering from shock and would come to terms with the verdict in time, but they hadn't allowed for the invisible link which bound her and Kirk. Only when she felt it sever would she accept that he was dead. Until then, she would go on searching as she had done these past years.

In that time she had used up most of her savings travelling all over Australia and taking out advertisements in newspapers. She had combed every hospital and clinic she could find, sure that there must be something seriously wrong with Kirk which had kept him from returning to her, or at least contacting her. At every turn, the answer had been dauntingly predictable: 'I'm so sorry, Mrs Wilding, but we have no record of anyone answering your husband's description being admitted here.' This was invariably followed by a shrug, a look of pity in the concerned eyes and sometimes even the suggestion that she go home, accept her widowed state and try to find someone else.

Find someone else! How could there be any other man for her after Kirk? Even their first meeting had had a fairytale quality. She had been returning home from England after visiting her family, and he was the captain of her flight. There had been some minor engine trouble which had necessitated their jettisoning some fuel and returning to Singapore. Nothing serious, the alarmed passengers were told. Then a tall, wide-shouldered man in his mid-thirties with a shock of blond hair tumbling over one eye under his uniform cap had strolled through the cabin, stopping here and there to reassure the worried passengers. In the economy section, he had paused at Erin's row of seats and looked down at her calm, smiling face. He told her later he had also been appreciating her gamin beauty created by broad, high cheekbones, a voluptuous mouth and wide hazel eyes fringed by chestnut lashes.

'Well, here's one passenger I obviously don't need to reassure,' he said warmly. 'Have you been through something like this before?'

The racing of her heart in response to his lopsided grin had nothing to do with their predicament. 'No, I haven't flown very often at all.'

'Then why so serene? Maybe the cause is catching. The other passengers could certainly use a little of your secret!'

To this day, Erin didn't know what had prompted her to be so completely honest with him. Until she met Kirk, she had been shy and awkward with men, especially when they were obviously so much in command of themselves. 'I know when I'm in good hands,' she told him simply.

He regarded her with astonishment and pleasure. 'I do believe you mean that, Miss . . .?'

'Warner, Erin Warner,' she supplied, 'and I did mean it.'

He touched two fingers to his cap in a quick salute. 'Kirk Wilding at your service. It's touching to come across someone with such complete faith in me.'

Her innate shyness caught up with her in a rush and she could feel her creamy skin reddening under his amused gaze. What was she thinking of, having such a conversation with a complete stranger? He had grinned at her sudden attack of shyness and saluted again, before making his way back towards the cockpit.

They hadn't remained strangers for long. The plane landed safely at Singapore and the passengers were offloaded while the trouble was rectified, then they were allowed to reboard to continue their journey to Sydney. While they waited in the airport lounge at Singapore, Captain Wilding had caught up with her. 'Can I buy you a drink, Miss Warner?'

She had accepted, and they spent a heady half-hour getting to know one another in the airport bar. Since he was on duty, Kirk only drank club soda, she remembered, but beyond that she couldn't have said what they talked about—or even if they talked in words at all. From the first, there had been a different kind of communication between them which sparked back and forth like electricity.

Erin had been nineteen when they married. Now she was twenty-four and understood that what they shared was a unique kind of sexual chemistry which could make them feel as if they were making love even over vast distances, without any physical contact. When they *were* together, the magic was total and devastating. Erin had never considered herself a sensual being, but with Kirk she was transported to dimensions of sensations which she had never dreamed existed.

In wonder, she commented to Kirk about the extraordinary sense of oneness they shared. It was as if they were one person in two bodies. Neither of them had any family in Australia—hers were in England and what relatives he had were in New Zealand, making the bond all the more precious to them both.

'We were meant for each other, Angel,' he had told her, and she had smiled at his use of the pet name he had given her. He said it was appropriate since their first meeting had been in the sky. 'Nothing will ever keep us apart,' he had promised her.

But something had—a bizarre turn of events neither of them could have foreseen when he made her that promise.

Three years ago, Kirk took his light plane up for a spin, as he called it, practising for a charity air show in which he planned to take part. Erin had stayed at home because she couldn't bear to watch him taking such risks, flying upside down and hurtling the plane into calculated stalls, only bringing it out of an apparent death dive at the last second. Such stunts might thrill the crowds who paid to watch, but to Erin, it was heart-stopping. When he was at the controls of the big commercial jets, it was different somehow. They didn't scare her nearly as much as the small planes Kirk flew on his days off.

Her fears had proved well founded. Since there were no witnesses, Erin never discovered what had caused Kirk to ditch his plane into the sea off the coast of New South Wales. The official thinking was that he had gone into a dive and been unable to pull out in time. Whatever the cause, his plane had been located in the sea on a shelf of rock a few miles off the coast. There was no sign at all of Kirk.

Sharks—that had been the unspoken explanation for the absence of a body, but Erin knew she would have felt something if Kirk had been taken in such a way. The link between them was too strong. She had even known when his jet had a near-miss with a private plane which had flown off course in the crowded skies over Sydney's international airport. That near-mishap wasn't reported by the media, but she had known about it and told him when he came home that night. His eyebrow had lifted slightly in the quizzical way she loved so much, but he hadn't really been surprised. The communion between them was something they took for granted by then. It also had its practical side. Kirk could never surprise her by returning home early. Somehow, she always knew and had a meal in the oven and candles on the table awaiting his arrival.

'Can't fool you for a minute,' he would laugh as he swung her playfully into the air.

'Not unless you stop sending me those radar signals of yours,' she joked in response.

Well, now he had. She had had no sense of his nearness for the last three years, in any of the places she had visited. Except for Sands Engineering. Even without the picture in the newspaper, she would have sensed that this factory was important to her as soon as she passed through its gates.

For luck, she touched the picture in her apron pocket, glad that she had been able to purchase a copy from the newspaper which had published it in their social pages. 'Industrial magnate Don Sands and his beautiful heiress wife, Leila Coventry, announce expansion plans for the Wattle Park Division of Sands Engineering,' the caption had read.

At the picture of the man unfurling a sheaf of drawings while a slight, blonde woman looked on, Erin's heart had all but stopped. The likeness was incredible but, more than that, her private radar was quivering as it hadn't done for years. Could this possibly be Kirk? If it was, why was he living under an assumed name and with—her pulses fluttered wildly at the thought—a woman who claimed to be his wife? Whatever it cost her, Erin had to know the truth.

Getting a job at Sands Engineering had been much easier than she expected. The personnel manager, Bert Halstead, had merely cast a leisurely look over her trim figure and shining chestnut hair and nodded. 'You'll do. Start Monday.'

She was bemused. It was happening so quickly. He hadn't even asked about her qualifications—not that her secretarial skills, which were impeccable, would be much use in a factory. But surely there was some sort of experience needed? 'What kind of work will I be doing?' she asked uncertainly, not liking the way Mr Halstead was looking her over with frank appreciation.

'That depends on you, darling,' he had leered. 'Play your cards right and who knows what job you could end up doing.'

Erin hadn't liked that at all. She found the man quite repulsive, but since he was the key to her getting a job at Sands Engineering, she had no choice but to smile agreeably, 'Thank you, Mr Halstead.'

'Bert, please. I have the feeling you and me are going to be ... er ... good friends.'

Not if she could help it, she thought grimly, but smiled and left as quickly as she could.

When she reported for her shift the following Monday, she found she was to work on the assembly line, turning out thousands of oddly shaped pieces of metal whose purpose she only vaguely understood. The factory made aircraft components, she was told, so she supposed the pieces of metal ended up inside a plane. This idea made her feel queasy, but she fought the sensation down. She should have expected that Kirk would gravitate towards some kind of aeronautical activity. Planes had been as much a part of him as breathing, so, whatever else might have happened to him, she didn't expect that to change.

With a start, she realised she had already begun to think of Don Sands as Kirk. She would have to stop that until she had more to go on. All she had so far was a newspaper picture of a man who bore a certain resemblance to her missing husband—and the feeling resonating inside her and which was growing stronger by the minute. This feeling, more than any logical evidence, was enough to convince her that she had found Kirk at last.

It was all she could do to work steadily at her monotonous job. Since Kirk had vanished, she had supported herself and her quest with a series of temporary secretarial jobs, and compared with them, this repetitive routine was mind-dulling. Still, remembering what was at stake, she made herself continue to lift each heavy metal sheet, feed it into the machine, and pass it along the assembly line to the next girl whose job was to shoot rivets into the metal.

Erin had been at the factory for a week which seemed more like a year, when Rosa, the Greek girl next to her on the line, gave her a warning nudge.

'Better get a move on. The big boss himself is watching us!'

The hairs on the back of Erin's neck rose slightly, but she willed herself not to look around, not yet. What if it wasn't Kirk? Then a voice spoke close to her ear and all her remaining doubts were swept aside in a torrent of remembered sensations.

'Hello. You're new here, aren't you, Miss . . .?'

'Wilding,' she said softly, not daring to look up to see what effect the use of her surname would have on him.

He didn't react.

'Erin Wilding,' she repeated.

There was still no flicker of response. 'Do you like working here, Miss Wilding?' he asked her.

This time she looked straight into his eyes, but there was no trace of recognition in them. At the sight of his familiar, gold-flecked grey eyes regarding her benignly, a lump rose to her throat and tears scalded the back of her own eyes. It took every ounce of willpower she possessed not to cry out his name, but until she knew more about what had brought him to this strange state, she dared not say anything.

'I asked you if you like working here,' he repeated.

'I . . . I haven't been here long enough to say yet. The work is . . . er . . . interesting.'

There was a hint of amusement in his expression as he looked back at her. 'Liar,' he said unexpectedly.

Her head came up with a jerk. 'What?'

'Nobody ever found an assembly line "interesting",' he told her. 'What are you doing here—slumming?'

She was genuinely baffled. 'I'm sorry, I don't know what you mean, Kir . . . Mr Sands.'

He didn't seem to notice her slip of the tongue. 'I think you do know,' he contradicted her. 'You don't look or sound like the average process worker. You wouldn't be an industrial spy, by any chance?'

She knew that her practised grooming and the expensive clothes she wore under her apron, legacies of better-off times, made her something of a misfit here, but she had never considered that she would be mistaken for a spy. 'No, of course not,' she denied hotly, feeling colour flood her cheeks.

Her consternation made him smile, and at the sight of that familiar grin, her heart turned over and she caught at the bench for support.

'Relax, I was only teasing,' he assured her. 'I hope you decide you like working here—when you've had time to make up your mind, of course.'

Then he was gone, leading the group of executives on the rest of their tour of inspection, his long strides forcing the others to scurry to keep up. Longingly, Erin stared at his broad back, noting how the muscles stretched the grey wool of his suit taut across his shoulders. He looked well, she thought—that was something at least. But what had she expected—a gaunt, emaciated figure, scarred by the ravages of illness? She realised that, unconsciously, it was just what she *had* expected, because it would have explained his long absence. Seeing him like this, so tanned and vital-looking, only confused her the more.

A throaty sound of impatience reminded her that the work was banking up and Rosa was waiting for her to catch up. To cover her inner turmoil, she busied herself feeding the metal into the press, but she was shaking so much with reaction that she fumbled her first few attempts to position the sheets correctly.

'Are you feeling all right, Mrs Wilding?'

She looked up to see the foreman watching her worriedly. 'I'm fine, thanks,' she said quickly.

'You don't look too good. Why don't you go and see the nurse during your tea-break?'

'Yes, I ... I'll do that,' she agreed. But when the whistle blew for the break she didn't head for the clinic. There was no medicine for the desolation of spirit which ailed her. Instead, she hurried out of the factory and stood in the sunshine, gulping lungfuls of clean fresh air while she tried to bring some order to her chaotic thoughts.

Sands Engineering was located at Wattle Park, one of the newer industrial estates on the outskirts of Sydney. When it opened, it was heralded as a model of environmental planning by the state government. Looking around, it was easy to see why. The factory building was set amid rolling green lawns dotted with tennis courts and a swimming pool for the employees, with a screen of tall poplars hiding the ugly expanse of car park from view. At the back of the factory building, the lawns sloped towards a river which was fringed by weeping willows and it was towards the river that Erin hurried. The tea-break was only fifteen minutes long and woe betide anyone who was late back, but she had to get away by herself to think, even if it was only for a few minutes.

She was as sure as she had ever been of anything that Don Sands was Kirk, no matter what he was called now. Yet he didn't even know her.

Desolately, she sat down on the grassy banks and let her thoughts flow with the swirling waters of the river. So she had found Kirk—what was she to do next? In all the long months of searching, she had never once stopped to consider what she would do when her search ended. If she had imagined the situation at all, she had pictured herself finding Kirk in some hospital, and nursing him back to health so they could take up where they left off. Never in her wildest dreams had she imagined he would have made a new life for himself in which she had no part, not even as a fond memory.

'Oh, Kirk, my darling,' she whispered to the rustling willow branches, 'if only you could tell me what happened to do this to you—to us!'

In the distance, she heard the whistle sound, signalling the end of the break period. She knew she should go back, but she couldn't, not yet. First, she had to see Kirk, talk to him and try to get through to him somehow.

The foreman believed she was ill—if she let him go on thinking that . . . it was out of character for her to take advantage of his concern, but she didn't see what else she could do. She scrambled to her feet and returned to the factory, where she explained her sudden illness to the foreman.

'Did you see the nurse?' he asked worriedly.

'I . . . er . . . no, not yet. I just sat outside to rest to see if it would help.'

'Then I'll take you to the clinic now.'

Erin looked around in panic. 'There's no need, really. I can find my own way.'

Luckily for Erin, an alarm bell sounded on one of the conveyor belts, indicating that something had jammed. The foreman smiled at her apologetically. 'Looks like I'm needed here. Are you sure you can manage?'

She nodded. 'Quite sure.' Before he could return, she picked up her bag and fled outside again. She felt badly about deceiving him when he meant to be kind, but this was something she had to do.

Going to see Kirk at his office was out of the question. She would have to run the gauntlet of secretaries and receptionists, and it was unlikely that they would let her in to see him. Whatever the problem, they would politely but firmly redirect her to the personnel manager or some other minor executive whose job it was to shield the top brass from employee harassment.

She couldn't go to his home for fear of running into Leila Coventry, the woman described in the newspaper as his wife. Erin's only alternative was to wait for him until he left the factory to go home in the evening. She knew she couldn't just hang around the main entrance. One of the security guards would be bound to want to know what she was doing there.

The car park! If she waited at Kirk's car she would be sure to catch him, no matter how late he decided to work.

She located his car, a maroon Mercedes, easily enough. It was parked in a space marked 'Reserved for D. Sands, Managing Director'. As she crouched low between the cars to keep out of sight of the attendant, she sent up a silent prayer that Kirk's car would be unlocked. It was and she breathed another prayer of thanks as she slid into the front passenger seat. Another blessing was the car's tinted windscreens which allowed her to see outside but concealed her from the view of anyone passing.

For what seemed like an eternity, she sat in the luxurious car, oblivious to the opulence of the leather-lined interior and figure-hugging bucket seats, praying that, tonight of all nights, Kirk wouldn't choose to work late.

The final whistle blew and almost at once a stream of people erupted from the main building. Laughing and joking, they scattered to their cars and the bus stop. Although she knew no one could see her through the tinted windows, Erin slid down in her seat, feeling as if every eye was on her. In less than half an hour the car park was almost empty, leaving only the executives' cars in their reserved spaces. She couldn't have much longer to wait now.

But it was another two hours before the creak of the car door and a cool rush of air against her cheek disturbed her. She sat up quickly. Despite the tension within her, she had managed to doze off in the comfortable seat, exhausted by the many sleepless nights she had endured since seeing Kirk's picture in the paper.

His eyebrow arched through his hairline as he caught sight of her and his gaze travelled slowly over the length of her body, making her wish she had woken in time to do something about her untidy appearance.

'To what do I owe the pleasure of this visit, Miss ... Wilding, wasn't it?' he queried and slid into the driver's seat beside her.

'Mrs,' she said automatically. 'I was waiting for a chance to talk to you.'

'And you apparently don't believe in office hours,' he said dryly.

'What I have to tell you isn't very ... appropriate for the office,' she stammered. Now that the moment was here, she found herself unexpectedly tongue-tied. What would his reaction be if she blurted out that she was his wife, whether he knew it or not?

He folded his arms and studied her with mild amusement. One would think he was accustomed to finding women waiting for him in his car at the end of a day! His next words, however, belied this impression. 'Mrs Wilding, I'm sure what you have to tell me is of the utmost importance to you, but since we've never met before today, I can't imagine what problem we could have in common.'

Far, far more than you know, Erin thought in anguish. Aloud, she said, 'Where were you three years ago?'

His look of amusement turned into disapproval. 'This sounds suspiciously like the third degree,' he growled.

'You don't know, do you?' she challenged him. 'Well, I do.'

He sighed deeply. 'How much do you want?'

Her eyes widened. 'How much? But I don't ...'

'It is money you want, isn't it?' he interrupted. 'The blank where my past ought to be is sufficiently common knowledge that it's to be expected someone comes along every now and then with a cock-and-bull story to fill the gap. Usually there's a child involved and I'm supposed to be the father. Is that your story, or have you come up with something more original?'

She shook her head, tears blinding her. 'No, it's nothing like that. I . . . oh, Kirk, I'm your wife—don't you remember me at all?'

'No, I don't remember you,' he said heavily. 'If we *had* met, I don't think I could forget a woman as lovely as you are.'

His index finger traced the line of her jaw with a feather-light touch which sent a shiver down the length of her spine. With all her being, she had yearned to experience his touch again, yet now she recoiled from it. He was touching her like this because he thought it was what she had come for, to be seduced by him in return for material gain. Well, it wasn't what she wanted, no matter what he thought. But how could she convince him she was telling the truth, when he thought she was just one more in an apparently steady stream of opportunists who had tried to take advantage of him? 'Don't, please,' she pleaded.

His expression was cold and unyielding. 'So now it's "don't", is it? I thought this was what you wanted. Or do you hope to do better by playing hard to get?'

She turned her head away. 'I'm not playing at anything,' she protested. 'You and I were married for two years, then three years ago you disappeared.'

'And you've been looking for me all that time—how touching! I don't suppose you have any proof of your story?'

This was a moment she had dreaded. 'While I was away last summer, following what I thought was a lead to my . . . your . . . whereabouts, my flat was burnt out. This is the only photograph I have left.' With hands that shook uncontrollably, she opened her wallet and showed him the blurred snapshot she had taken when they were on holiday on the Barrier Reef, earlier in their marriage. 'It's not very clear,' she apologised unhappily.

He hardly glanced at it before he turned back to her. 'About what I'd have expected, but somehow I thought you might do better than that.'

'It doesn't matter, since you don't believe me anyway,' she said in a tone which was barely audible. She started to get out of the car, but he moved faster, flicking a switch on the dashboard so that the locks on all four doors sprang shut at once.

'No, you don't—not so fast!' he cautioned. 'You haven't told me your price yet.'

What was the use? Nothing she said would convince him that she wasn't a cheap confidence trickster. 'I told you, I don't have a price,' she tried anyway.

'Tell you what, I'll pay you anyhow,' he offered. Erin looked at him in puzzlement, then stiffened as he moved closer to her. As she realised what he meant to do, she scrabbled ineffectually at the locked door, then was pressed against the seat cushion by the full weight of his body as he brought his lips down on hers. Suddenly, nothing else in the world mattered beyond the fact that she was in Kirk's arms once more. She could feel their magic working even if he couldn't and she surrendered herself to it willingly, pressing her lithe body against his with the hunger of three years' abstinence. His body arched in response and, as his lips continued to devour hers, his hand sought the curve of her thigh and stroked it gently. She moaned softly as wave after wave of desire washed over her. He pressed one hand against her hair, moulding her eager lips to his, exploring the inside of her mouth possessively. When his other hand moved higher along her leg, she felt the fires of passion rising within her.

'Oh God, Kirk, it's been so long,' she gasped.

'No, it hasn't, and you know it,' he said coldly, breaking away from her with cruel suddenness.

'Then why did you do that?' she appealed, her senses still reeling from the abrupt parting.

He ran a distracted hand through his thatch of blond hair, loosening the errant curl so it fell across his forehead, causing a pain like a knife thrust to tear into her at the sight of it. 'Damn it, I don't know. I just had to, that's all.'

So at least a trace of their old magic still remained and he *was* affected by it, however much he tried to deny it! She knew he was as aroused as she was by the contact. Maybe, just maybe, she had managed to open a tiny chink in his self-assurance. If so, it might be the first step to help him regain the memory he had apparently lost.

He gripped the steering wheel with both hands, his eyes fixed unseeingly on the row of poplars in front of them. 'You're a witch,' he said distantly. 'Is that your game—bewitch me until I can't resist your demands, whatever they may be?'

'No, it's nothing like that,' she said with a calm she didn't feel. 'I . . . I've only ever kissed one man like that before in my life . . . and that was my husband.'

He stared at her in astonishment. 'You expect me to believe that after the way you've just responded? Oh, lady, you're a cool one, all right! I just wish I knew what you were up to.'

'I've told you, but you refuse to believe me.'

'Do you think I could be married to a woman like you and just forget her?' he asked scornfully.

'If something sufficiently traumatic happened, yes, I do,' she argued. 'If you had been injured, it might cause you to lose your memory, and I think that's what happened the night your plane crashed into the sea off Port Macquarie.'

He looked at her sharply, his expression shedding its rigid mask of disbelief for the first time. 'What made you mention Port Macquarie?' he demanded.

'That's where your plane was located.'

At once, he relaxed and broke into a harsh laugh. 'My God, for a moment there you almost had me believing you, but you could have read about it somewhere.'

'Read what? I only know about it because of the crash.'

'For goodness' sake, do you have to sound like a broken record? It's common knowledge that my wife, Leila, has a beach house at Port Macquarie. That's where I collected the crack on the head that wiped out my memory—not from any plane crash.'

'I think I'd better go,' Erin said dejectedly. For a second, she thought she had been making some progress, but she had only compounded his impression of her as a confidence trickster. 'Please, open the car doors.'

'No, I'll drive you home. Where do you live?'

'Manly, but you don't . . .'

'Yes, I do. I live at Newport Beach, so it's on my way. It's too late for you to catch a bus anyway.'

She sat silent and miserable as he manoeuvred the powerful car out of the parking lot and on to the expressway. She should be thankful for these extra minutes in his company, but she only wanted to get away somewhere to lick her emotional wounds. She didn't know what she was going to do next. 'I suppose I'm out of a job now,' she said after a while.

'What for? To fire you now would only make it look as if there was some truth in your story. Where there's smoke . . . and all that. No, report for work as usual tomorrow.'

As she climbed out of the car outside her block of flats, Erin couldn't resist asking the question which had been burning in her brain as they drove the last few miles. 'Tell me one thing.'

'What's that?'

'Are you in love with Leila Coventry?'

His brows knitted together in a frown. 'What in hell kind of question is that?'

'Call it female curiosity if you like. Are you?'

'None of your damned business,' he growled, and reached across to pull the passenger door shut. Then he slammed the car into gear and roared away up the hill with a screech of tortured tyre rubber.

As she watched him go, she felt a sense of elation steal over her. She might not have made much progress, but there was a little. She had found Kirk at last and he was not immune to the chemistry between them, whatever he thought. His reaction told her that he wasn't in love with Leila Coventry even though they were supposedly married. The heiress had probably been a safe harbour when he needed one, nothing more. That meant there was still a place for Erin in his heart if she could reach him. She only hoped she was strong enough to see it through.

CHAPTER TWO

NEXT morning, Erin awoke with a lighthearted feeling, and at once the reason came rushing back to her. She had found Kirk at last! Then she frowned as she remembered how remote he had been, with no recollection whatever of their marriage. Well, his mind might not remember her, but his body did, she would swear to it after the way he had responded when they kissed in his car. Perhaps she could reawaken the passion they had once shared and, through that, the rest of his memory.

But what was she going to do about Leila Coventry, the heiress who claimed to be Kirk's wife? Somehow, she had a feeling Leila could provide answers to many of Erin's questions. If that was the case, she wasn't going to welcome Erin's arrival on the scene. She would have to tread warily where Leila was concerned, Erin resolved, but she had found Kirk, and for now that was all she cared about.

When she reported for her shift at the factory, her shining eyes and glowing skin caught the attention of the foreman. 'Whatever the nurse gave you yesterday, tell her I'd like some of it,' he told her.

'Some of what?' she asked, puzzled. Then she remembered that she was supposed to have been taken ill yesterday. 'Oh, that—I just needed a few hours of rest, that's all.'

'It's a flaming miracle!' the foreman grumbled goodnaturedly as he went off about his duties.

Erin smiled after him, feeling in harmony with the whole world, although she still couldn't help glancing at the closed door to the executive offices every now and then, hoping to catch a glimpse of Kirk.

During the morning tea-break, she joined the other women from her section at a big laminated table in the employees' canteen. 'Ah, here comes the Big Boss's darling,' Rosa teased, her smile taking any malice out of the remark.

Erin looked at her in alarm. Did she know something? Then she realised she was being teased because of the way Kirk had singled her out during his inspection yesterday. 'I can't help being irresistible,' she said with forced gaiety.

'You have to admit, he did seem taken with you, Erin,' a girl called Linda contributed.

'Waste of time—he's married,' another girl chimed in wistfully.

Erin wondered what they would say if she told them he was, indeed, married—to her. Like Kirk himself, they probably wouldn't believe her, she thought sadly. She busied herself unwrapping the sandwich she'd brought from home to have with her coffee, so the others wouldn't see the blush which she could feel staining her cheeks. 'You're imagining things,' she said into her coffee cup.

Rosa winked. 'Play your cards right and he might invite you to the Spring Ball.'

The comment reminded her of the lecherous suggestion the personnel manager had made when he hired her, and she shuddered involuntarily. Then the rest of Rosa's remark caught up with her. 'What do you mean, the Spring Ball?' she asked, feeling a sudden surge of interest.

'Nothing that would concern the likes of us,' Linda responded. 'It's a classy do for the management. We peasants have our own shindig every Christmas. This one's all champagne and long dresses.'

'Kir . . . Mr Sands,' Erin amended quickly, 'would he attend this ball?'

'Of course. He and Miss High-and-Mighty Coventry are the host and hostess. All the top brass are expected to attend. It's considered proof of loyalty to the firm, or some such.'

'I see. Thanks,' Erin mused, hardly noticing the curious stares she drew from the others. She drained her coffee cup and stood up. 'I'm ready to go back.'

'Relax, the whistle hasn't blown yet,' Linda told her. 'Don't be too much of an eager beaver or they'll expect the rest of us to be the same!'

The others couldn't be expected to understand the sense of excitement which was gripping Erin as an idea began to form in her mind. If she could only get herself invited to the Spring Ball, she could dance with Kirk. In his arms, with their special chemistry at work, she would have perhaps her only chance of awakening his memory.

She could think of only one way to make her plan work, and the prospect made her feel ill at the very idea. The personnel manager, Bert Halstead, had already expressed a personal interest in her. If she could only make him think she returned his interest, he just might take her to the Ball. He wasn't married; that much she had gleaned from the factory's constantly buzzing grapevine, so he would be in need of a partner. There was a chance he wouldn't want to be seen with a mere employee, of course, but if he thought there was a pay-off at the end of the evening for him, he might be persuaded.

Erin began to put her scheme into action the next time the personnel manager made his rounds of the factory. Until now, she had all but ignored him, answering as briefly as possible when he spoke to her, but being careful not to encourage his attention.

Today, however, she could hardly wait until he reached her bench. Her heart hammered wildly in her chest and her hands were so clammy with perspiration that she had trouble working her machine, but she forced herself to appear outwardly calm as he approached her.

'Hello there, darling, everything all right?' he asked.

Instead of giving her usual curt response, she turned a beaming smile his way. 'Hello, Mr Halstead . . . er . . . Bert. Everything's fine, thank you for asking.'

'All part of my job,' he muttered, sounding surprised at her change in attitude. 'That's what I'm here for, to see to the welfare of the personnel.'

Especially the female ones, Erin thought spitefully. However, she made sure this thought didn't show on her face. Instead, she fluttered her long, silky eyelashes at him. 'There is one little thing you can do for me, Bert,' she breathed.

When he moved closer, their hips touched and she had to steel herself not to move away. 'What's that, Erin?'

'I . . . I'm not sure whether I'm doing this job exactly right,' she dissembled. 'Perhaps you would show me.'

Strictly speaking, this was the province of the foreman, but she felt sure that Bert Halstead would never pass up such an opportunity. Predictably, he placed an arm around her shoulders and drew her closer while she tried not to stiffen in his repulsive embrace. 'Stand closer to the machine, like this,' he said softly, and his breath came in quick gasps in her ear. 'Why don't you stop by my office after work and I'll give you a few more tips that might help.'

'Why, thank you, Bert,' she smiled, breathing a sigh of relief when he finally moved away from her. Her body felt soiled where his pudgy hands had touched her. Still, she had achieved her first goal—a private audience with him. Now she had only to get out of his office with an invitation to accompany him to the Spring Ball—and her virtue intact.

Later, as she made her way through the deserted offices, she couldn't resist peeping into Kirk's lavish suite. Beyond the empty outer office she could see into his private domain, and she caught her breath when she glimpsed his fair head bent over some paperwork. His long fingers moved effortlessly over the surface of an electronic calculator. She let her gaze rest for a long moment on his hands, while she drank in the sight of the deft movements and remembered the feel of that same hand caressing her hot skin.

'Ah, there you are, Erin. So come in.'

She turned her attention to Bert Halstead, who had evidently mistaken her hesitation outside Kirk's office for uncertainty as to which way to go.

'This way, my dear,' Bert urged, and came out to lead her into his own office. He kept a hand under her elbow while he closed the outer door. Erin felt trapped. Maybe she had made a mistake even coming here. Then she concentrated on what she had come here to do. So much depended on convincing Bert that she was interested in him and prepared to be cooperative in time.

He saw her hunted look and patted her shoulder with his free hand. 'Don't look so worried, Erin. The days when managers ate staff whole are long past.'

'Not where you're concerned,' she muttered to herself. The way his tongue constantly moved over his thick, pale lips, he looked as if he could eat her right now, perhaps not for dinner, but certainly as a bedtime snack.

'What did you say?'

'Oh . . . er . . . I was just admiring your office. It's . . . er . . . very comfortable.'

He steered her to a leather-upholstered couch which took up most of one wall. While she sat down, he moved to a bar set up in one corner. 'We're both off duty now, I'm sure you'd like a drink,' he stated rather than asked.

Erin nodded, knowing she would need the stimulus of the drink to give her the nerve to carry out her plan. He poured a nip of brandy for her and a more generous portion of Scotch for himself, then came to sit down beside her on the couch and handed her her drink.

'Now, tell me about this problem you're having with the work.'

She shifted sideways so she was facing him to ward off any attempt of his to sidle closer. 'It's not really a problem,' she improvised, 'it's just . . . well, I'm new to factory work, and . . .' she tailed off and took a quick, steadying gulp of her brandy.

'But not new to the business world, I'm sure.' He reached across and placed a hand on her knee. 'For instance, you've obviously worked out that there are other ways besides hard work to climb the ladder of success.'

At his touch, her blood turned to ice in her veins, but she forced herself to smile. 'It didn't take me long to work out who really runs things around here,' she said. At least that was the truth, even if not in the way Bert would think she meant it.

'I knew you were a smart girl,' he grinned. 'You'll go a long way with an attitude like yours!'

He reached for her, but she had been expecting the movement and stood up at once, to wander with apparent casualness across the office to his desk where she had spotted a large, gilt-edged card.

He watched her, a petulant expression on his face, obviously unsure whether his timing had been faulty or she had outmanoeuvred him. 'What are you doing?' he asked irritably.

'You can learn a lot about a man from his office,' she murmured, casting a careless eye over the papers scattered across the desk. Finally, she picked up the invitation. 'Is this for the Spring Ball?' she asked innocently.

'What if it is?'

'All the girls have been talking about it. They'd give their eye teeth to be asked,' she gushed.

'Yes, well, it's for executives only.'

She sighed prettily. 'So they tell me. It's a pity you're not allowed to invite an employee to partner you.'

Bert downed his drink in one swallow and his face flushed with annoyance. 'What do you mean—not allowed? No one tells me what to do around here! I can take anyone I choose.'

'Then you *will* take me?' she gasped, her eyes shining.

He looked confused. 'I . . . er . . . that is . . .'

'Oh, thank you, Bert,' she enthused. 'At least at the Ball, we won't have the constant worry that we might be interrupted, will we?'

Guiltily, he followed the direction of her gaze towards the door and she knew he was thinking of Kirk—or Don Sands, as he knew him—still working at his desk nearby. Then Bert's eyes grew warm as he looked back at her. 'You're right, the Ball will be something to look forward to, won't it?'

Before he could say any more, Erin skipped quickly to the door and let herself out, leaving him staring after her in bewilderment.

Outside, in the main office, she stopped to catch her breath, then ran all the way to the women's restroom, where the enormity of what she had done caught up with her. For the next few minutes she clung to the basin, retching uncontrollably. Then, white-faced but feeling better, she left the factory and caught her bus home.

The days until the Spring Ball seemed endless and

she had to contend with an impatient Bert Halstead, who grew more amorous by the day.

'How can you put up with that creep?' Linda asked her at last.

'I can handle him,' Erin said confidently, but inside, she was far from confident. He fully expected her to respond to his advances at the Ball and she had no idea how she was going to cope when he demanded his 'payment' for taking her. For the moment, she was pinning her hopes on being able to dance with Kirk at the Ball. As host, he would have to dance with each of the women in turn, she was sure.

On the night of the Ball, she dressed with infinite care in an outfit which was one of the last gifts Kirk had given her before he disappeared. Luckily, she had taken it with her on the fateful weekend when her flat was destroyed by fire, so it was one of the few dresses she still possessed which Kirk might remember. The outfit comprised a cream off-the-shoulder satin shirt and matching full-length skirt worn with a cream shawl threaded through with gold, and spindly metallic sandals.

The result was gypsy-like and provocative, especially with the bare shoulder revealed by the unusually cut blouse. Kirk had brought the outfit back for her from Hong Kong. She recalled how pleased he had been that she liked it, even though it was more daring than anything else she owned. She had worn it often to please him, and now she hoped against hope that it would trigger some trace of memory when he saw her in it again tonight.

After a moment's hesitation, she wound her chestnut hair into a loose knot on top of her head, teasing a few wisps of curl free around her face to accentuate her high cheekbones. She intended to use every weapon in the book to capture Kirk's attention tonight!

Her budget rarely stretched to cosmetics, but a dusting of ginger blusher and two shades of tawny eyeshadow were enough to make the most of her natural assets. Her one extravagance was a tiny flacon of expensive French perfume and she dabbed some of it sparingly on to her pulse points and the cleft between her breasts, grimacing as she noted how little was left in the bottle.

The impatient clamour of a car horn broke into her thoughts. That would be Bert come to pick her up—the right expression in the circumstances, she thought ruefully. Not wanting to give him an excuse to come up to her flat, she picked up her purse and shawl and hurried down to the waiting car.

Chivalry was not one of Bert's virtues—in his eyes, women were good for one thing and one thing only. He made no move to get out and help her into the car, only reaching across to open her door from the inside. As they drove, he made no comment about her appearance, but his leisurely appraisal told her he was weighing up how easily the garment could be removed later when he claimed the payment she had hinted would be his for taking her to the Ball.

The foyer of the luxury hotel was already thronged with lavishly dressed couples by the time they drew up. Bert handed his car keys to the attendant, then strode ahead of Erin into the glittering ballroom, greeting several people he knew on the way. She hardly noticed any of them, being too busy scanning the crowd for signs of Kirk. His tall, commanding figure should make him easy to spot even in this mêlée. With a stab of disappointment she realised he wasn't here yet.

For appearances' sake, she supposed, Bert handed her a glass of champagne and stayed beside her as they circulated. She was sure none of the other executives of Sands Engineering recognised her as a lowly hand from their own factory.

'Well, hello there. Your fairy godmother turned up, then, did she?'

There was no mistaking that velvet tone, and a thrill coursed through her at its sound. She spun around and nearly collided with the broad expanse of Kirk's chest. He looked breathtakingly handsome in his midnight blue dinner suit and snowy white ruffled shirt which accentuated his deep, even tan.

'I'm sorry, I didn't catch that,' she said sweetly, although she had heard his reference to her Cinderella status perfectly well.

His eyes twinkled. 'Oh no? It wasn't important, then. You look very lovely tonight, by the way.'

'And my pumpkin coach and white mice are in the parking lot,' she rejoined gravely.

He threw back his head and laughed in the way she remembered painfully well. 'Touché! Truce, then?'

Willingly, she matched his smile with her own. 'Truce.'

Someone was signalling to him from across the room and he shrugged ruefully. But before he left her, he caught her elbow and pulled her close so her nostrils were assailed by the spicy tang of his aftershave beneath which was a musky tint of maleness which brought back floods of memories. 'Dance with me later.'

It was more of a command than a request, but Erin's heart sang. Was the chemistry working on him more strongly than she allowed for?

'For God's sake, stop making cow eyes at Don Sands,' growled Bert at her elbow. He had a fresh Scotch in his hand and from his flushed face she gathered he had already drunk more than was good for him.

'I wasn't doing any such thing,' she defended herself.

'Oh no? I saw that mooning look on your face. Just

remember who you came with—and who's coming back to your flat with you when this is over!'

With this blunt reminder of her obligation to him hanging over her head, she was unable to enjoy a mouthful of the banquet. Course after course was placed before her and she only nibbled around the edges of each dish, feeling relieved when the toasts and speeches began. She had trouble concentrating on what was being said, because her eye was constantly drawn to Kirk at the head table. Beside him, sat a regal-looking blonde woman who Erin guessed must be Leila Coventry. A thrill of hatred coursed through her at the sight of the petite, self-assured woman who claimed to be Kirk's wife. What right had she to sit beside him, bending her head to his and laughing at something he said? Despite the crowd around her, Erin felt achingly lonely.

At long last, the band began to play and couples drifted on to the dance floor. Erin steeled herself to dance with Bert, but luckily, he was too preoccupied with the liberal supply of wine and liqueurs to pay her much attention, far less be able to negotiate a dance floor. Several of the other executives asked her to partner them and she did so woodenly, then finally gave up the pretence of having a good time and sat beside Bert in tense silence. Just when she had decided Kirk had forgotten his promise, he appeared at her side and led her on to the dance floor. This was the moment she had been waiting for, and she moulded herself to him eagerly.

He looked down at her in surprise. 'You dance very well,' he complimented.

'We always did make a good pair,' she could have said, but instead she concentrated on making love to him with every curve of her body, pressing her thighs against his muscular ones and lifting her face to his so she could feel the soft wind of his breath on her cheek.

As she moved deliberately against him, she could feel his surge of response and he held himself rigid as a tremor of emotion passed through him. 'My God, you don't mess about, do you?' he asked in a low, vibrant tone.

'All's fair in love and war,' she reminded him.

'Which is this, then?' he demanded.

'You tell me.'

'I'll tell you something—if you don't stop this, I just may shock all these very proper people by taking you right here on this dance floor!'

She pretended shocked surprise, but inside, her heart was singing. So he could feel the chemistry working, too! 'Why, Mr Sands—and you a married man!' she flirted.

'I may be married, but I'm not made of stone,' he cautioned. 'The way you come on to a man makes it very hard to resist.'

The bubble of happiness which had been cocooning her burst abruptly. It wasn't the chemistry at all. He thought she behaved like this with every man she met! Shattered, she made as if to turn away from him, but he caught her around the waist and kept her pressed to him. 'Oh, no, you don't. You interest me very much, Mrs Wilding. I'd like us to have a little talk—what say we wander out on to the terrace for some fresh air?'

She had no choice but to nod abjectly and allow him to tow her through the throng. She was conscious of the curious stares that followed their progress through the room and out on to the moonlit terrace.

Gently but firmly Kirk led her to a stone bench and pushed her down on to it. 'Stay there. I'll get us a drink,' he ordered.

'No, *you* stay here,' Erin wanted to cry out. She didn't want a drink. She wanted to press home her advantage and see, at last, the dawning awareness in those grey eyes before she lost her chance. But he was already moving back inside, towards the bar.

'So this is where you've been hiding!' Her heart sank when Bert wove his way unsteadily on to the terrace, with a glass still clutched in his hand. 'What did Sands want with you?' he demanded.

Bert must have seen her come out here with Kirk. 'N-nothing,' she stammered. 'He . . . we . . . just wanted to talk.'

A sneer curled the edges of Bert's mouth. 'I'll bet he did! But I know what kind of talk he had in mind.'

Erin shook her head violently. 'You're wrong, Bert.'

'Am I? I saw you on the dance floor with him. You seemed to forget you were out in public and not in his bedroom.'

'That's enough!' She was so incensed that she lashed out unthinkingly, and her first awareness of what she had done came when she drew her hand back and saw the livid red marks of her fingers on his face. 'Oh, I'm sorry, Bert, I . . .'

'Save it!' he ordered savagely, setting his glass down carefully on the bench. 'You shouldn't have done that, you know.'

'You shouldn't have said such terrible things to me!'

He smiled, but without warmth. 'Lady, just wait and see what I can say—and do.' Like vice grips, his hands closed around her bare arms and he hauled her to her feet so she was pressed against his chest which heaved with the intensity of his rage. The alcohol on his breath made her gasp as he pulled her closer. Desperately, she struggled in his grasp, but she was no match for his solid bulk and he laughed at her futile writhings.

Thinking furiously, she tried to make her voice sound reasonable. 'Let me go, Bert. People are watching.'

He glanced over his shoulder, then glared back at

her. 'They can't see us here in the shadows. Anyway, you should have thought of that when you were making an exhibition of yourself on the dance floor with Sands!'

Moving swiftly for one so heavy, he grasped the elasticised neckline of her off-the-shoulder dress and pulled hard. The elastic snapped and the neckline sagged, exposing her breast to his raking glance. She started to scream, but he covered her mouth with his other hand, stifling any sound. Then he grasped her exposed breast and squeezed it cruelly, so she cried out with the pain. Slowly but inexorably, he forced her backwards, deeper into the shadows, and she was in no doubt as to what he intended to do next. How could she have been such a fool as to think she could 'handle' an animal like him?

Then unbelievably, he was wrenched away from her and thrown bodily against the opposite wall, where he slumped, breathless and glowering with rage.

'Are you all right?' Kirk demanded, turning to her.

Erin nodded dumbly, too shocked by her narrow escape to think straight.

'Why shouldn't she be, she was asking for it?' Bert sneered, recovering his power of speech.

'No woman invites rape,' Kirk said evenly, but Erin could see from his laboured breathing and hands which clenched and unclenched that he was controlling his temper only with a great effort.

'Oh no? Why not ask her what price she was willing to pay for her ticket to the Ball?'

Kirk's jaw muscles worked, but he kept his hands rigidly at his sides. 'Get out of here, Halstead,' he said in a low tone, but there was no mistaking the threat in it.

Hastily, Bert scrambled to his feet and disappeared back into the ballroom. When he had gone, Kirk turned to Erin. 'You'd better do something about your dress.'

She bunched the material in one hand and pulled it up so it covered her breasts but, with the elastic broken, she had to hold it to prevent it slipping down again. 'You can't think I wanted this to happen?' she whispered hoarsely.

He sighed with exasperation. 'Frankly, I don't know what to think about you. When we danced in there, I told myself your response must be due to some irresistible attraction on my part—not unflattering for a man, you'll agree? But now—well, it looks as if you do use your body as a passport to getting your own way.'

'That's not true,' she cried miserably.

'Then Halstead was lying when he suggested that you'd promised him your favours in return for bringing you here?'

Erin hung her head, wishing she could lie to him but knowing that he would find out the truth somehow. 'I did let him think that,' she confessed, 'but it was only so I could have a chance to be with you.'

'We're back to that again, are we? For God's sake, woman, you're very beautiful and you seem to have plenty of intelligence. If you want to, you can make something of your life instead of throwing it away like this!'

She stared at him, aghast. He was pitying her! He thought she was a parasite whose attempt to persuade him that he was her husband was just another of the shady schemes she lived by. How was she to convince him he was wrong? She had hoped that being in his arms on the dance floor tonight would stir some trace of memory, but she had failed miserably. Instead of reminding him of what they had been to each other until three years ago, she had made herself look like an unscrupulous petty criminal and a man-chaser.

In despair, she turned her head to the wall and was

startled when he placed a hand under her chin, to turn
her gently back to face him. 'I meant it when I said
you were very beautiful,' he said softly. 'There's
something about you that . . .'

'Yes, go on,' she urged.

Kirk looked deep into her eyes. 'I wish I knew what
it was. All I know is the more I see of you, the harder
I have to work to remind myself that I'm a married
man.'

'Then perhaps you could use a timely reminder,'
drawled an indulgent voice. Framed in the ballroom
doorway was Leila Coventry.

Kirk turned and broke into a smile. 'Leila!'

The other woman's eyes narrowed as she took in
Erin's torn dress and wild-eyed appearance. 'This is
hardly your style, Don, so I gather that Bert Halstead
has been up to his tricks again.'

'You gather right. I'm going to have to do
something about that bastard.'

'You can't. For the same reason he's got away with
it before. None of the girls he has bothered are willing
to make an official complaint.' She directed her
haughty gaze at Erin. 'Am I right?'

An official investigation into tonight's fiasco would
only hinder any further chance she might have of
seeing Kirk. 'No, I . . . I don't want to complain. I'm
all right, really.'

Leila's glance at Kirk clearly said, 'I told you so'
and she rubbed her hand seductively along Kirk's
forearm. 'You've done your White Knight act, darling.
I'll take care of Miss . . .?'

'Erin, please.' For some reason, she was oddly
reluctant to give her full name to Leila. She could
recognise it and, with her wealth and power, might
make it impossible for Erin to see Kirk again.

'Erin, then. Since you can't go back into the
ballroom in that condition, I'll take you out the side

way and put you in a taxi to take you home. Don, will you fetch this poor child's things?' He went back inside and returned a moment later with Erin's purse and wrap which he handed to her.

'This is very kind of you both,' Erin murmured, feeling anything but grateful. She was sure Leila only wanted to get her out of the way as quickly as possible.

Her opinion was confirmed when the older woman placed an arm around Erin's shoulders and led her out through the shadowy gardens towards the front of the hotel. 'Don't misunderstand my husband,' she said silkily into Erin's ear, 'he doesn't really need any reminders as to whom he's married. I'm sure he just wanted to bolster your ego after what happened tonight.'

'I'm sure he did,' Erin said dryly, and could almost feel the look of surprise which Leila directed at her.

As they emerged into the brighter lights of the hotel forecourt and waited for the hotel doorman to hail a cruising taxi, Leila studied Erin more closely. 'Haven't I seen you somewhere before?' she queried.

It was possible that she had seen Erin's photograph in the newspapers during the search for Kirk's plane. She could also have seen Erin at work. 'I'm employed by Sands Engineering,' Erin said quickly, feeling it was better to encourage this line of thinking and steer Leila away from discovering who she really was. If Leila knew, Erin guessed she would stop at nothing to keep her and Kirk apart. Why she should have such a conviction, Erin had no idea, but the more she thought about it the more she believed that Leila was somehow involved in Kirk's disappearance and reappearance as Don Sands.

The taxi drew up just then and the doorman held the car door open for her. Thankfully, Erin climbed in. 'Thank you for your help,' she said stiffly.

Leila waved a hand dismissively. 'Think nothing of

it, Erin.' She leaned closer so she could talk to Erin
through the car window. 'I'd be more careful in future
if I were you. Our Bert is a terror when he's aroused.
Maybe you should think about changing jobs.'

You'd like that, wouldn't you? Erin thought to
herself as the car moved away. But not because Leila
cared about Erin's wellbeing. She looked as if she
would deliver Erin to Bert personally if it suited her.
Rather, the suggestion had been made because Leila
sensed that Erin was a threat to her. Well, she would
soon find out how right she was!

CHAPTER THREE

IF it wasn't for the pressing need to pay the rent and keep the fridge stocked, however meagrely, with food, Erin would have thought twice about going back to Sands Engineering at all after the scene with Bert Halstead last night.

She shuddered when she thought about it now. If Kirk hadn't intervened in time, Bert Halstead would have . . . she gulped back a sob at the memory. It was no good dwelling on that awful moment. She would do better to concentrate on avoiding a repetition, which seemed distinctly possible, since she was sure a man like Halstead would not take kindly to being humiliated as he had been last night by Kirk.

Most importantly of all, her job at the factory provided the only means she could think of to be near Kirk so she would have a chance of restoring his memory.

Not that she had been very successful so far, she thought unhappily. He had proved he was aware of the physical bond between them, but his strong sense of honour was getting in the way. Despite her inner confusion, she smiled wryly. She had never imagined she would have cause to curse Kirk's idealism, which included a deep respect for the sacrament of marriage. If only she could make him see that his loyalty was entirely misplaced!

Slowly she drew out the blurred snapshot of him and stared at it, feeling a stab like a knife thrust, lance through her. 'Oh, Kirk, why can't you remember me?' she implored, wondering afresh what could have happened to create such a barrier between them in his mind.

This kind of thinking would get her nowhere, she told herself sternly, and began to dress for work and tidy up the little bed-sitter. In her present state, she didn't feel she could face breakfast, so she broke an egg into a glass of milk and whipped it to a foamy texture, then sipped it. The last thing she needed right now was to make herself ill through neglect.

When she arrived at the factory, she noticed that some of the other girls were staring at her. As soon as she sat down at her bench, she found out why she was the object of their curiosity.

'You're wanted at the main office right away, Mrs Wilding,' the foreman told her.

She looked at him in alarm. 'What for?'

He shrugged. 'I don't do the hiring and firing around here, lass. I just mind the store.'

Hiring and firing? Heavens above, was she to be sacked over the scene with Bert Halstead last night, even though Kirk knew it wasn't entirely her fault?

'Better tidy yourself up first,' the foreman advised her as she stood up to go.

Erin nodded distractedly, her mind dwelling on the possibility that she could lose her job—may already have lost it in fact.

To steady her nerves, she took the foreman's advice and went first to the rest-room where she loosened the pins which held her hair neatly in place while she was working. She brushed it furiously into its usual shining curtain. The physical act made her feel calmer and her hands had stopped trembling by the time she came to touch up her lipstick, which she usually didn't wear to work. Finally, she untied her apron and rolled it into a ball which she pushed into her locker, possibly for the last time, then made her way to the main office.

The receptionist raised an eyebrow at the sight of Erin, as if to ask what she was doing in such hallowed territory. 'Yes?' she queried haughtily.

'Someone from the management sent for me,' Erin explained, feeling foolish. In her confusion she had forgotten to ask the foreman which executive had summoned her. Oh God, she hoped it wasn't Bert Halstead. Was this his way of exacting his revenge on her?

'I was the one who sent for you,' a velvety voice said, and Erin looked up into Kirk's grey eyes.

At once, the receptionist melted into a picture of sweetness and charm. 'Of course, Mr Sands. Go right through there, miss,' she urged, pointing towards the door through which Kirk had already gone.

Aware that the receptionist was staring after her curiously, Erin made her way through the outer offices and into Kirk's private office. He was seated on the front of his desk with one leg swinging free, while he glanced through a file.

'You wanted to see me?' Erin asked nervously.

His tone was impersonal. 'Yes, Mrs Wilding, please sit down.'

She perched nervously on the edge of an upholstered visitor's chair and waited for Kirk to finish reading his file. He might be able to treat her like a stranger because of his amnesia, but she found it almost impossible to treat him the same way. Nevertheless, she would have to if she was to remain here, near him. When she could stand the waiting no longer, she blurted out, 'No matter what you think, I'm not slumming, you know. I have my rent to pay and myself to support.'

He looked at her in astonishment. 'If this is a plea for a raise in your wages, I'm afraid . . .'

'Oh, no,' she cut in hastily. 'I just want to make sure you understand that I really need this job.'

'Not this job—*a* job,' he corrected her. 'With your qualifications, you shouldn't have any problem finding a position, most likely at twice the salary you've been getting here.'

If he intended to fire her, he was going about it in a very strange way, she mused. 'What do you know about my qualifications?' she couldn't resist asking.

He tapped the file with a long finger. 'It's all in your personnel record. You're wasted on the assembly line, you know.'

She braced herself to hear him say that she was too good for her present job and that's why he was letting her go. 'If I'm to be dismissed, why don't you just say so and get it over with?' she challenged him.

He laughed, and the familiar throaty sound made her want to weep with the futility of it all. 'What do you mean—dismissed? Why do you think I brought you in here?'

'Wasn't it to fire me on Bert Halstead's recommendation?' she asked, mystified.

'Good grief, no! I wouldn't order a cup of coffee on Halstead's recommendation. No, actually I wanted to offer you a promotion of a sort. You see, my personal assistant left to get married on Friday and I thought you'd be ideal for the job.'

'Me?' she asked. It was the last thing she had expected from him, and she could hardly believe it was happening. Here was a golden opportunity for her to work alongside Kirk. Surely if she was in his company every working day, he would start to remember her?

'Yes, you,' he was saying. 'Normally, I would have advertised, since we don't usually have someone with your background already on the payroll and available. As well as that, it wouldn't be fair to ask someone to give up a secure job to work here for a couple of months. Your present job would still be open after that if you wanted it, so you wouldn't actually be giving anything up. And with the reference I could give you, you would probably get a much better job if you wanted.'

As fast as he had raised her hopes, he was dashing

them again. 'Two months? What happens then?' she asked.

'I'm surprised you haven't heard it on the grapevine,' he explained, unaware of the agitation growing within her. 'In two months' time, we're merging this company with our opposite number in the United States to form an international consortium. Under the terms of the merger, I'll be going over there to help head up the new company, so I'll only need an assistant here until Leila and I head for California.'

Erin tried to keep her tone level but could not entirely conceal the dread she felt, as she asked, 'How long will you be staying in California?'

'For good, I expect. They're much more centrally located to serve our world markets, so I'll probably leave a general manager here and run the overall show from the States.'

She felt sick with horror at what she had just learned. In two months, Kirk would be going to live in another country for good! She could never afford to follow him there, even if she could arrange the necessary permits and visas. Once he went to America, she would never see him again, but that wouldn't stop her from being tormented by the knowledge that he was there, believing he was the husband of another woman. It would be like a living death, she knew, because however far apart she and Kirk might be, as long as he lived Erin would consider herself married to him in mind and body. She fought back a sob of despair.

'That's an odd reaction to a job offer,' he commented. 'I realise it's only a short-term proposition, but surely it's better than the work you're doing at the moment?'

'Yes, of course,' she agreed tonelessly.

'Then why the hesitation?'

'I have the feeling your ... Miss Coventry ...

wouldn't like you hiring me to work in your office. Last night she suggested that I should look for another job as it was.'

His mouth twisted into a humourless smile. 'Did she now? Well, we have to get one thing straight. Leila may run the Coventry Corporation, but she doesn't run Sands Engineering, even though Coventry is the parent company. That was the agreement when I took over here, otherwise I wouldn't have touched the job. This place was just a run-down nuts and bolts factory two years ago when I recommended that the Corporation ought to take it over, and I got them the first big contract which set them on their feet. So Leila doesn't tell me how to run things around here. Understood?'

'Yes, of course,' she agreed. It was obviously a sore point with him that the Corporation belonged to Leila and so did this factory, however indirectly. She could well believe it of Kirk. As long as Erin had known him he wasn't happy unless he was master of his own destiny, which was why he was so temperamentally well suited to flying the big jets. Up there in the sky, he used to tell her, he was totally in command, responsible for every decision made and the life of every person on board. She couldn't imagine him willingly giving command of his life over to anyone, especially not to a woman like Leila Coventry.

'Then you'll take the job?' Kirk asked.

What choice did she have? At least this way, she had two months to be near him and try to restore his memory. If she hadn't managed it in that time, perhaps she would have to face the fact that she never would. In that event, it was probably better if she didn't have to endure the agony of seeing him every day, being near him but never *with* him. If two months was all she had, she would have to use every minute of it to try to reach him because, after that, nothing would matter anyway. 'Yes, I'll take it,' she said resolutely.

'Good girl!' he enthused. 'I have the feeling we'll make a good team. Welcome aboard, Erin.'

It was the first time since his disappearance that he had used her first name and she felt a thrill of pleasure course through her. He was only using it because she was his new assistant, but it still brought back a flood of tender memories, all the same.

'There's only one condition,' he said seriously. 'But we may as well get it straightened out once and for all.'

'What's that?'

'You have to promise me you'll drop this charade that you're my wife. I don't want you to mention it again, not even to me. Is that understood?'

She stared at him, wide-eyed. 'Oh, but . . .'

'I need that promise, Erin.'

'But why?'

'Because I think you're much too beautiful and capable to be indulging in petty fraud. If you'd tried such a story on anyone but me, you could have landed in gaol. I want to give you a chance to make something of your life.'

Now she knew why he hadn't referred to the scene in the car again. 'But it wasn't a story, I swear,' she breathed. 'Oh, Kirk, aren't you curious about who you are—or were before you knew Leila?'

His expression became stony. 'I was, at first,' he admitted. 'When Leila and I returned from our honeymoon, she was talking with an acquaintance who happened to be a freelance journalist. He wrote a sensational story about how Leila Coventry's new husband couldn't remember his past. He wanted to use my photograph too, but I drew the line at pictures of me headed "do you know this man?". I'm surprised you didn't read the story at the time.'

After Kirk had disappeared, Erin had been too

distraught to read a newspaper or look at a television set for months, so it was little wonder that she had missed it. His next words proved that it wouldn't have made much difference even if she *had* read the story.

'This was the result,' he said grimly, and dumped a file of letters into her lap.

The first one she took out was written in sloping feminine handwriting on pink paper which still retained a trace of flowery perfume. In the letter, the woman explained how relieved she had been to read the story about Kirk, and to discover what had become of him. They had been lovers, she wrote, and a child had resulted. Not that she wanted any money from Kirk, she stressed, but it had been a struggle maintaining the child since his father disappeared. If Kirk wanted to help, cheques could be sent to the address at the top of the letter.

'Go on, read some more,' Kirk urged. 'They don't get any better.'

He was right, she found out. There was one from a woman claiming to be his ageing mother; two more from girls who said he was the father of their children; and one in language so crude and explicit that Erin blushed scarlet as she read the suggestions in it. She looked up at him helplessly. 'These people must be sick,' she said.

He laughed hollowly. 'That's pretty good, coming from you!'

She gestured hopelessly towards the letters. 'You can't think that I'm the same as . . . as these?'

'Can't I?' he demanded. 'No one knows the hell I went through after I woke up at Leila's beach house. Even though she showed me photographs, a marriage licence and other documents, they meant nothing to me. I was a man without any past. I could have been a criminal a murderer . . .'

'Or already married?' Erin suggested gently.

'Or already married. How was I to know? If it hadn't been for Leila sticking by me, I would have gone mad. By the time these letters began to arrive I was desperate for any scrap of information about my past, so I followed them all up meticulously. Leila even interviewed some of the writers herself.'

Erin knew what he was going to say next. 'They all turned out to be frauds?'

'Yes, every damned one of them. The last letter was the most convincing. The child even looked like me, except for one thing.'

'And what was that?'

He shook his head in disgust. 'All it took was a simple blood test to prove that I couldn't have fathered her child.'

Erin spread her hands wide in a gesture of frustration. 'This doesn't mean *I* have to be lying. I could be the only one telling the truth.'

'You still don't understand, do you? I can't afford to take that risk any more. I've had so many bitter disappointments that I had to make up my mind to quit before I went off my head. The doctors tell me my memory may return one day, or it may not. For now, I've got to live with the possibility that I may never know the truth about my past.'

In the face of what he had shown her and told her, she understood why he was so unwilling even to listen to her side of things. Once bitten, twice shy, was the rule, and it seemed he had been bitten many times. 'I'm sorry, I had no idea,' she whispered.

'How could you? Can I take it that you'll give up trying to convince me that there's something between us?'

She looked down at her hands for a moment then faced him squarely. 'No, I won't. You're asking for something I just can't give you. You *are* my husband, whether you believe it or not, and I would rather die than deny you.'

Kirk stood over her, exasperation written in every line of his face. 'What do I have to do to get through to you?' he appealed.

'Kiss me,' she invited.

He stared at her in amazement. 'What?'

'You heard me. I give my word not to cry rape.'

'What the hell will kissing you prove?'

Her heart hammered wildly, but she forced herself to remain outwardly calm. 'If you can kiss me and still tell me that there's never been anything between us, then I'll give my word not to mention it again,' she vowed. She was staking everything on the chemistry which had always existed between them. If it failed her now, she had just thrown away her last chance to convince Kirk that she was telling the truth.

Kirk regarded her steadily for a long moment, as if weighing up her offer, and she ran her tongue along her parted lips, more from nervousness than from any attempt to be seductive. He mistook her gesture for the latter and bent his fair head towards her.

If the kiss he bestowed on her in the car was sweet, this was heady beyond measure, and her senses began to swim. At first, he kissed her with almost clinical expertise, then his blood seemed to catch fire along with hers and he forced her backwards until she felt the hardness of the wall at her back. She couldn't decide whether the wall or his body, bearing down on her, was the firmer. He had filled out a little in his executive role, but it was all hard muscle, and she marvelled at the power in his body as it drew her towards him like a magnet.

Excitement built to a crescendo inside her as his lips wandered more and more eagerly over her lips and throat. His touch was like flame and there was exquisite agony in her upper arms where his fingers dug into the tender flesh. Nothing in the world mattered beyond the fact that she was in Kirk's arms and his lovemaking was endowed with the full force of the magic they had once shared.

He had to feel it—he had to. This was no mere animal lust such as she had experienced at Bert Halstead's hands. This was the nirvana of two souls in such total harmony that they could live and breathe as one.

The telephone shrilled and he pulled away abruptly, staring at the phone as if it was an alien thing. Then he looked back at her in a mixture of awe and confusion.

She waited tensely, her body still quivering with the after-effects of his lovemaking. 'Do you still want that promise?' she asked almost inaudibly.

His eyes bored deep into hers as if searching for answers there to the questions she knew must be tormenting him. 'I should, by Heaven,' he ground out. 'I should get rid of you now before you destroy what little peace of mind I possess!'

'But you won't, will you?' she asked, feeling the first faint wellings of triumph inside her.

'No, I won't, God forgive me.' He turned away from her and from the self-loathing she glimpsed in his expression before he did so, she knew he was hating himself for this moment. He believed he was married to Leila, yet he had given in and kissed Erin with undisguised passion. By his own strict moral standards, his action was unpardonable.

'Please don't condemn yourself,' she pleaded.

He gripped her shoulders and shook her slightly. 'Why shouldn't I? I'm a married man. I should send you away right now, instead of even discussing it.'

Erin tossed her head back defiantly. 'Then why don't you?'

His unwilling answer, torn from him, told her all she needed to know. 'Because I can't, damn it all! I don't know why, but I can't.'

His hands were unsteady when he picked up the phone which had been ringing the whole time. 'What is it?' he barked into the receiver. He listened for a moment, then looked at Erin in anguish. 'Of course she can—send her in.'

The door swung open at once and Leila Coventry flounced in, looking annoyed at being kept waiting in the outer office. She was impeccably dressed in a white linen trouser suit with a red straw picture hat and shoulder bag, making Erin acutely conscious of her own dishevelled state. 'Don't you answer your phone any more, darling?' Leila asked Kirk, then froze as she caught sight of Erin standing near the filing cabinet in one corner. 'What's *she* doing here?'

'Erin is my new assistant,' Kirk responded. 'I appointed her this morning until we leave for the States.'

'Scraping the barrel a bit, aren't you?' Leila asked abrasively.

Tiredly, Kirk looked from one woman to the other. 'She's very well qualified, as it happens. Check the file if you like. She's had plenty of experience.'

'Oh, I'm sure she's very experienced,' Leila hissed, and there was no mistaking what kind of experience she implied. 'I just hope she knows her place, that's all.'

'Is there something I can do for you, Leila?' Kirk asked, distracting her.

Leila perched gracefully on the edge of his desk, crossing her pencil-slim legs at the ankle. 'No, nothing special. I just wanted to say cheerio to you before I left. My plane goes at three. Of course, if you'd rather I didn't go, I would be happy to put it off.'

'No, don't do that,' Kirk said a shade too quickly. 'I'm sure your sister-in-law will appreciate your company while she gets over her operation.'

'If only she and Tom didn't live in the mulga,' Leila sighed.

'I wouldn't call a property the size of Texas the mulga,' he laughed, easing some of the tension in the air.

Erin began to feel like the proverbial fifth wheel. Besides which, it was agony to have to stand there and see Leila being so proprietorial towards Kirk. She coughed, attracting their attention. 'I'll go to lunch now, if I may. When do you want me to start work here?' She still couldn't bring herself to call him anything but Kirk. She would rather call him nothing at all, even though it sounded rude to her own ears.

'Oh yes, Erin, by all means have your lunch. Report back here at two and I'll brief you on the paperwork we have to do for the merger.'

Thankfully, Erin escaped from his office and made her way towards the staff canteen. She had been too preoccupied this morning to pack a lunch for herself, but she decided, in the light of her promotion which was bound to carry a higher salary, she would treat herself to a meal in the canteen.

After Kirk's reaction this morning, she felt lighter in spirit than she had for some time. She had given him the opportunity to order her out of his life for ever, and he hadn't taken it. 'Because I can't,' he had confessed reluctantly. He didn't know yet what it was that bound them so tightly together, he only knew, subconsciously, that it was important to him. Now all she had to do was help him remember what it was.

When she reached the canteen, the girls from her old section were already seated at their usual table. Erin collected a tray and selected a salmon salad, bread roll, slice of apple pie and glass of milk from the self-service bar, and carried them to the table.

Rosa looked up at her in surprise. 'I didn't think you'd still be talking to the likes of us,' she said half-seriously.

'Why ever not?'

'It's already common knowledge that you've been moved into Mr Sands' *private* office,' Linda told her, emphasising the adjective.

That grapevine again! 'Well, I'm trained as a secretary,' she said defensively. 'Anyway, it's only a temporary position until he goes to America.' She didn't know why she should be explaining herself to these women who were, after all, only acquaintances, but she felt she should scotch any rumours before they got started. Her relationship with Kirk was already complicated enough without adding gossip to their problems.

However, it seemed she was already too late. 'Wish *I'd* been smart enough to get myself invited to the Spring Ball,' Linda put in. 'I hear you didn't so much dance with Mr Sands as pour yourself all over him. It certainly seems to have done the trick!'

The malice in Linda's voice brought tears springing to Erin's eyes. 'Why are you being so cruel?' she asked. 'I didn't ask for this job.'

Rosa put a reassuring hand on her arm. 'Don't let them get to you. They're only jealous.'

Rosa was right, of course. Still, if this was typical of the gossip already spreading around the factory, how long could it be before it reached Leila Coventry's ears and she gave Kirk an ultimatum to get rid of Erin?

Worry over this aspect had taken most of the joy out of discovering that she was to work with Kirk. By the time she reported back to the office, she was in the depths of despair. This time, the receptionist waved her through to what was now Erin's office, although the smile the other woman gave her never quite reached her eyes.

To her acute disappointment Erin found that Kirk had been called away to a meeting. However, true to his word, he had left a file on her desk which filled her in on all the details of the coming merger. As well as asking that she read through the file, he had left some letters on the dictaphone for her to edit and type ready for his signature. He would be back before she left the office for the evening, his note stated, and he asked that she wait until he returned in case his meeting generated any urgent paperwork.

It didn't take her long to fall back into the office routine, and it was heavenly to have a task which stretched her mind again, after the monotony of the assembly line. The details of the merger were complex and she had to read parts of the file over several times before she felt she had a good grasp of the situation. That done, she began to work on the letters for Kirk. In between, she took several phone calls, so it was late afternoon by the time she had completed her assigned tasks, and the receptionist had already poked her head around the door to say that she was going home. 'Coming?' she asked.

'I have to wait for Mr Sands,' Erin replied, and winced at the knowing look on the other girl's face. There wasn't much she could do about it, but she wished she hadn't made Kirk the target of innuendo. He didn't really deserve that.

'Good, you're still here,' Kirk commented as he came back in and saw she was still at her desk. 'This is Mr Burrows from California. John—my assistant, Erin Wilding.'

'How do you do, Mr Burrows,' she murmured.

He looked her up and down appreciatively. 'Delighted to meet you, Miss Wilding.'

'Come and join us in here, Erin, and bring your notebook,' Kirk instructed as the men went into his private office.

When they were seated around his desk, he explained, 'At this afternoon's meeting, we made a few significant changes to the terms of the merger. Mr

Burrows and I have to spell them out in legally acceptable form and write them into the agreement so we can telex them to California tonight, for approval from their end.'

The American smiled warmly at her. 'I hope this won't keep you from a date, Miss Wilding.'

She saw Kirk frown at this, but whether it was because Mr Burrows was obviously taken with her, or because he was waiting to hear her answer, she wasn't sure. 'Oh, no, I'm free tonight, luckily,' she answered lightly, hoping Kirk would take this as a hint that she wasn't always. If she could make him jealous, it just might help bring back his memory. She had so little time that almost anything was worth a try, she had decided during the afternoon while she was waiting for him to come back.

The meeting turned out to be a lengthy one and her shorthand, while not exactly rusty, had fallen into disuse, during her spell as a factory worker, so she had to concentrate to keep up with what the men were saying. After more than an hour of parties of the first part, and parties of the second part, her head ached and her eyes had begun to water from staring at her notebook.

'That's it, then,' she heard Kirk say at last, and she gave a sigh of relief. 'Can you handle a telex machine?'

She nodded, hoping that she was alert enough to remember how after the strain of the meeting. In her last few temporary positions, she'd had little occasion to use a telex, although she supposed it was one of those skills once learned, never forgotten.

Fortunately she was right, and it took her only a few minutes to familiarise herself with the type of machine used by Sands Engineering.

While the men watched, she typed in the alterations to the merger agreement, thinking with satisfaction of how her instructions were being received by a sister machine half a world away.

When she sat back at last, Mr Burrows beamed his approval. 'You're a wonder, my dear! You sure you can't persuade your boss to bring you back to the States with him?'

She smiled wryly. 'I don't think so.'

'Well, since I may not have the chance to see you again, perhaps you'll do me the honour of having dinner with me, since it's partly my fault that you've been kept working so late.'

'Oh, that's not necessary,' she assured him. 'I didn't mind, honestly. Besides . . .'

She had been going to say that she wasn't particularly hungry after having a larger-than-usual lunch, but Kirk got in ahead of her. 'Besides, she's already promised to let me buy her a meal as a thank-you for staying late,' he said flatly.

After this morning, she had been sure he would want to put as much distance between them as humanly possible. Perhaps their chemistry had been working strongly enough to make him curious about her, after all.

'Isn't that right, Erin?' he asked pointedly.

'Of course, I . . . I'd forgotten.'

Mr Burrows regarded them curiously. There was obviously something going on between them, but he couldn't work out what it was. Since the American deal also involved the Coventry Corporation as the parent company of Sands Engineering, he couldn't help but know that Kirk was married to Leila Coventry. Erin sighed heavily. The gossip would spread even further afield after this, and Leila would hear about it sooner rather than later. Erin wished she could think of something to say that might defuse the situation, but it was already too late.

Mr Burrows winked heavily at her as he took his

leave. 'You work on that boss of yours, mind? See if you can't persuade him to let you come Stateside with him. You'd make a real California girl in no time!'

'Goodnight, John,' Kirk told him firmly, and closed the office door behind him.

'Why did you say we had planned to have dinner together?' she asked as soon as they were alone.

'Do you need a reason? I already said it's a thank-you for staying late.'

There was a sharp crack as the pencil she'd been holding snapped in two. 'Why don't you admit that there is something between us?' she implored. 'You must feel it, or else why were you jealous of John Burrows asking me out tonight?'

He ran a distracted hand through his wavy fair hair. 'Was I jealous?' he asked in surprise.

'It sure looked that way to me,' she confirmed.

'Now you mention it, I suppose that's what I did feel,' he admitted, bemused 'It's almost as if . . .'

'As if what?' she prompted.

'Nothing,' he said with an air of finality. 'Get your coat, and I'll buy you that dinner I promised you.'

CHAPTER FOUR

THE restaurant he took her to was crowded and noisy and they discovered they would have to wait for a table to become vacant.

The owner was profuse in his apologies. 'If you had given me half an hour's warning ...' he said unhappily.

'It's all right, Marcel, I've told you—we only just decided to come ourselves,' Kirk assured him. 'We'll have a drink in the bar while we're waiting.'

The man smiled his relief. 'Splendid! I'll reserve the first vacant table for you, Monsieur Sands.'

Since there was a small queue ahead of them, this told Erin how highly the management valued Kirk's custom. She worried that there would be talk if they were seen together in one of his regular haunts, and she said as much to Kirk when they were seated at the bar sipping pre-dinner cocktails.

He cocked an ironic eyebrow at her. 'Worried about my reputation, Erin? Relax, I often bring business contacts here, male *and* female.'

Still, she couldn't relax completely and she half expected Leila to walk in at any moment, even though she knew the heiress was hundreds of miles away in the country by now. 'I have an idea,' she said at last, 'my flat isn't very far away—why don't we go there for dinner?'

He stared fixedly at the row of exotic bottles lined up along the back wall of the bar and she knew he was remembering this morning's encounter and wondering how far he could trust himself with her.

'I promise not to try to seduce you,' she said huskily.

'Isn't that supposed to be my line?' he growled back.
Then he downed his drink in one swallow and stood
up. 'All right, let's go. But remember—you're the one
who made the promise, I didn't.'

This comment sent a shiver of delight through her.
What exactly did he mean—that he hadn't promised
not to try to seduce *her*? 'Oh, Kirk, you did that a long
time ago,' she said to herself as she followed him out
to the car.

'You realise we've probably ruined Marcel's evening,' he told her as they drove towards her flat. 'He'll
never believe that I didn't mind about being kept
waiting.'

'He probably won't believe that I'm a business
contact either,' Erin said ruefully, and was aware she
had said the wrong thing as soon as she saw his mouth
tighten into a grim line. She half-turned in the car
seat. 'Please don't torment yourself,' she begged. 'We
aren't doing anything wrong.'

'Oh no? My wife's out of town and I'm driving to
the home of my secretary long after we should have
gone our separate ways. What would you make of that
in Leila's shoes?'

'She doesn't have to know,' said Erin in a low voice.

His expression turned sneering and she knew all his
disgust was directed inwards, at himself. 'So now I'm
going behind my wife's back as well,' he said. 'It gets
better and better.'

It was too much! She could understand his own
feelings of self-disgust because he believed he was
cheating on Leila. But Erin had no cause to feel
ashamed of being with him, whether he knew it or not.
She was his wife, no matter what Leila had told him,
and what documents she had produced. If anyone had
cause for feeling ashamed it was Leila Coventry,
certainly not Erin Wilding! Fury gave her the courage
to round on Kirk. 'I promised not to lead you astray,'

she seethed, 'so if you're worried about your precious code of honour, why don't you just drop me at my door and go home alone like a dutiful husband?'

His hands tightened their grip on the steering wheel and his knuckles whitened. 'You know very well why I won't do that.'

'And why might that be?' she provoked, although she already knew the answer.

'For the same reason I didn't throw you out of my office this morning,' he said tonelessly. 'Because I can't and you know it. Maybe I was right when we met in the factory car park, when I said you were a witch and you would cast a spell over me to get your own way.'

'You don't really believe that, do you?' she insisted. 'It's just easier to accept than the idea that the woman you've trusted so implicitly for the last three years might have been lying to you.'

He brought the car to a screeching standstill which almost threw her through the front windscreen until she was restrained by her safety belt. He leaned towards her and for a moment she feared he was going to hit her for her last remark, then he slumped back into his seat and placed both hands on the steering wheel. 'It's so simple for you, isn't it? You know who you are and what you want from life. Can you possibly imagine what it's like *not* to know? To have a black, yawning abyss where your past ought to be? Every second person you meet seems to have the right to theorise about who you are and where you came from. Well, I've had about all I can take of that, Erin. Leila's been the one constant in my life through it all—can you understand that?'

'I understand that you've been terribly hurt by your experiences in the last three years,' she concurred. 'But so have I. While you've been wondering who you are, I've also been wondering ... where my husband was, what he was doing and even if he was alive at all. The police and the divers who found the plane all worked hard to convince me my husband was dead, but I wouldn't accept it because of one thing. You seem to have lost that one thing, but it's kept me alive and functioning for three years and I'm not going to let anyone destroy it now.'

'What are you talking about—what thing?' he wanted to know.

'Hope, Kirk,' she stated, using his real name and not caring how he reacted. 'Hope is what kept me going, and no one is going to take it away from me!'

Without a word, he restarted the car and this time they drove in thoughtful silence until they reached the block of flats in which Erin lived. She could almost hear him mulling over what she had said, but she was determined not to take back a word of it.

'This is a very pleasant little nook,' he told her when she showed him into her flat. He looked around appreciatively at the small decorating touches she had added to make the place seem more homelike. She hadn't had a real home since Kirk disappeared, but she couldn't help herself trying to make the succession of rented places in which she'd lived seem more welcoming. Luckily, she was blessed with a flair for decorating, so she was able to employ a little money and a lot of imagination to achieve spectacular results.

The flat itself was hardly worthy of the name, comprising a cooking alcove with a small table and two chairs for eating, a bathroom, a balcony overlooking the seashore, and a large room divided into two by an archway across the middle. One half she had reserved for sleeping, with most of the space being taken up by a double bed which came with the flat. The other half of the room was furnished with two armchairs, a coffee table and her one luxury, a stereo record player. Sadly, most of her records had been lost in the fire which destroyed her previous flat, but she had been able to replace several of her most cherished albums.

'You pick out some music while I put the steaks on,' she told Kirk. Shedding her jacket, she went into the kitchen and began taking out the ingredients for their meal. There was enough steak for two if she only had a small piece, and she always kept salad ingredients on hand. While the steaks were sizzling in a pan, she tossed the salad in a cheap wooden bowl which, nevertheless, looked attractive.

To the strains of a violin concerto, Kirk watched her from an armchair where he had made himself comfortable. 'You look very domesticated doing that,' he commented.

'I *am* very domesticated,' she rejoined, 'as you should remember.' At once, she saw his face darken. 'I'm sorry, I didn't mean that—it slipped out.'

'Forget it.' He stood up and stretched luxuriously. 'I don't suppose your budget runs to wine?'

She grimaced. 'I'm afraid not.'

'Well, mine does. And since you're supplying the meal, the least I can do is contribute the drinks. Where's the nearest liquor supplier around here?'

'Turn right as you go out of this building and walk half a block to the next intersection. It's on your left next door to the newsagent.'

'Any preferences?'

Erin thought for a moment, but her knowledge of wine was very limited. 'Surprise me,' she said at last.

When he had gone, she moved the small dining table out into the centre of the living room and draped it with a hand-embroidered cloth, then set it with cutlery and dinnerware, wishing she had something more glamorous than department store plates to set out. Kirk was actually here with her, as if nothing had changed, she marvelled. She felt like celebrating.

Except that a great deal had changed, she reminded

herself grimly. Still, the war was far from lost. On
impulse, she took out a pair of candles she had bought at
a sale recently and set them on the table, then hunted
around for a box of matches. Candles on a table should
always be lit, she recalled reading somewhere.

The steaks were almost cooked, so she spread a
length of French bread with butter sprinkled with
fresh herbs, swathed it in aluminium foil and popped
it into the oven to warm. Then she stood back and
surveyed her handiwork with satisfaction.

The doorbell pealed and she hurried to let Kirk in.
'Marcel couldn't have done better,' he laughed as he
saw the table. He handed her a bottle wrapped in
brown paper, through which she could feel the chill of
the wine.

In the kitchen, she located the corkscrew and drew
the bottle out of its bag, then stared at the label in
astonishment.

'Don't tell me I chose a wine you don't like?' said
Kirk in concern.

'No,' she corrected in a strangled voice. 'Actually
you picked our ... that is, my ... favourite wine.' It
was a German Liebfraumilch, the same brand they
had drunk on their honeymoon and decided to make
'their' wine from then on. Each time they had
something to celebrate, they had opened a bottle of
this particular wine. She hadn't tasted it since Kirk
disappeared and now, to have him choose it of his own
accord—was there a chance he retained some traces of
memory after all? 'What made you choose this wine?'
she asked.

He shrugged. 'I don't know. I wish I could say it
was the year, or the side of the hill the grapes were
grown on. But I've never bought it before, so it isn't
any of those things. It just seemed to suggest happy
times, that's all.'

Erin turned away, ostensibly to tend to the steaks,

but it was really so he wouldn't see the tears which were filming her cheeks.

'You should have let me peel the onions for you,' he joked as he caught sight of her face when she brought the meal to the table.

She forced a smile to her lips, glad that he had supplied his own explanation for her tears. 'Next time, I'll do that,' she promised.

The meal progressed pleasantly after that as both of them steered the conversation along carefully neutral paths, avoiding anything remotely personal. Sipping the fruity wine brought back a flood of sweet memories to Erin, but she made herself react normally and smilingly agreed when he remarked that he had chosen well, however illogical his reasoning.

At last, he pushed his chair away from the table. 'I'm almost glad that Marcel didn't have a table for us!'

Erin was too, but not for the same reasons. Methodically, she began clearing the table and declined his offer to help her. 'I'll put a record on before I do the dishes,' she told him. 'It won't take me long and we can listen to the music together while I work.'

'Aye, aye, cap'n,' he smiled, and took his wine glass over to one of the armchairs. Stretched out there, he looked so much at home that her heart constricted in protest and she bent quickly to the task of choosing a record. Her hand hovered over an album of Grieg favourites. Dared she? Then she recalled how little time she had left to stir Kirk's memory, and resolutely slid the record out from its sleeve, placed it on the turntable and switched it on.

While the record spun in, she moved the table back to the kitchen, this time accepting Kirk's offer to help her. By the time the living room was tidy again and she had started on the dishes, the orchestra was playing the first of the lovely 'Elegiac Melodies'. She knew this record practically by heart. Kirk had given her their first copy of it on an anniversary, because they both loved the music so much. Any moment now, they would come to the haunting strains of 'The Last Spring', which she and Kirk had considered uniquely their own.

Elbow-deep in soapy water, she paused dreamily as the piano and strings played the opening section with its nostalgic suggestion of cool Norwegian fjords. Her heart felt as if it would burst from her chest as the music swelled and swelled to a peak, emphasised by rolling drums. The music evoked such strong memories of her life with Kirk that it was no wonder she had been unable to face playing it since the day he disappeared.

'For God's sake, shut that off!'

Startled, she swung around to see Kirk slumped in his chair with his eyes closed and his face contorted with pain.

She hurried to kneel at his side, no longer hearing the music she had been so absorbed in moments before. 'What is it, what's the matter?'

His fingers dug convulsively into the arms of the chair. 'I said shut that blasted music off! Or have you gone deaf?'

Hurt beyond words, but frightened by his strange behaviour, she jumped up and lifted the arm off the record. At once, silence pervaded the room. 'Is that better?'

'It will be in a few minutes.'

'You mean you've had turns like this before?' He nodded and grimaced at the pain the movement caused him. 'Then you must know what to do. Is there something I should get for you?'

'In my jacket pocket,' he ground out with an effort, 'there's a prescription. Didn't have time to get it filled.'

'Don't worry, I'll do it for you right now. There's an all-night chemist near where you bought the wine.'

She found the prescription and, stopping only long enough to pick up her purse, raced down the stairs and out into the street where she flew on wings of fear to the chemist's shop. Although it was no more than a few minutes, it seemed an age before the chemist returned with a jar of capsules and she paid for them. 'Thank you,' she smiled distractedly, then hurried back to the flat and Kirk.

He was still half lying in the chair when she returned. Hastily, Erin filled a glass with water and took it to him with the tablets. 'How many should you take?'

'Two.'

She spilled them into a hand that shook with fear, and offered them to him with the water, supporting his head with one hand while he swallowed. 'Better?' she asked.

'Give it time,' he whispered. 'I thought I'd seen the last of these attacks.'

'How many have you had?' she probed anxiously.

He opened his eyes slowly and seemed able to focus on her again. 'Maybe half a dozen in all,' he told her tiredly. 'Mostly, they occurred in the early days after the boating accident.'

Boating accident? she thought blankly, then remembered that Leila had told him that was the cause of his amnesia. 'What brought it on now, do you think?'

'Remembering,' he said with a wry grin, 'or, rather, trying to. Every time I try to get a grip on my past, I get one of these blinding attacks of pain.'

'Were you doing that now?' she asked him tensely. 'Remembering, I mean?'

'I wasn't trying to, no. But there was something in that music you played just now that tore through me like a bullet.'

'Music does that sometimes,' she said, trying to contain the surge of hope she felt. 'It can bring back memories of people and places. Did the music tell you anything about yourself?'

Kirk shook his head and winced with pain. 'Only that there's something terribly wrong—I just can't put my finger on what it is.'

The 'something wrong' must be his relationship with Leila, Erin was convinced. But she dared not probe too deeply for fear of starting another attack of pain, and she couldn't bear to see him go through that again if she could prevent it. 'Are you all right now?' she asked instead.

He let his head drop back against the armchair. 'Apart from feeling as if I've run the four-minute mile, I'm fine. The tablets tend to make me a bit drowsy, but at least the pain is going. The doctors tell me it will probably go for good when I get my memory back—if I ever do.'

'Thank goodness!' she breathed, then drew a sharp breath as he began to struggle out of the chair. 'Where do you think you're going?'

'I have to get home and sleep this off,' he said unsteadily.

'I'm not letting you get behind the wheel of a car like that,' she said firmly. 'You can sleep here, in my bed.'

He looked at the double bed which was the only visible sleeping accommodation, then back at her again. 'And where will you sleep?'

'I keep a folding stretcher in the wardrobe, I'll sleep on that,' she lied. She knew that if she told him she planned to sleep curled under a blanket in the armchair, he wouldn't agree to take the bed, and he was much too ill to drive home.

At any other time, he might have seen through her strategy, but tonight he was much more affected by the attack than he was letting on, she was sure. Groggily he staggered to the bed and stretched full length on top of the covers. He was asleep when his head had barely touched the pillow.

For a long time she stood looking down at him tenderly, all the love she had for him transparent in her eyes. Then she carefully removed his shoes and tie. He still didn't stir, so she took a deep breath and began to remove the rest of his clothing. Without the restriction of his suit and shirt, he would sleep much more comfortably and he looked as if he could use all the rest he could get.

He was a big man and his dead weight resisted her first attempts to undress him. Luckily, he was so deeply asleep that he didn't react to her struggles, and eventually he lay on the bed naked except for a close-fitting pair of black underpants. With his athletic build, he looked like the model for a life painting class, and Erin wished she had the skill to capture him in this pose. Instead, she concentrated on storing up the memory of this moment, and ran her hand lovingly over the curve of his thigh, noting how the muscles knotted under her hand. The fine hairs on his legs rustled as she caressed him, and an ache gathered deep in the pit of her stomach. Suddenly she felt a need for him that was almost palpable and she had to fight an urge to crawl into the bed beside him and cling to him for comfort. More than that, her senses yearned for his possession as she had last known it three years ago. She wanted him to touch her, hold her and take her as his wife, calling her his Angel again. Yet all she could do was watch him helplessly, and a tear of frustration rolled down her cheek.

Angrily she snatched her hand away. She was acting like a sex-starved old maid! Resolutely, she turned her back and busied herself folding his clothes neatly over the back of a chair. Then she tiptoed to her own chair and curled up there, turning so she could keep a watchful eye on him from where she sat. After a while, the evening chill made her shiver, so she went into the bathroom and stood for ages under the hot shower. Under the circumstances, maybe it should have been a cold one, she thought moodily, as she wrapped a terry towelling robe around her glowing skin and returned to the living room.

Kirk still hadn't stirred, so she covered him with a blanket, then snapped off the light, pulled a rug over herself and settled down to sleep in the armchair.

The dream she had had many times since Kirk disappeared came back, but this time it was more vivid than ever before. Kirk was with her and they were once more living as husband and wife.

They were walking together along a sandy beach which stretched endlessly ahead, and the dream was so vivid that she could feel the strong warmth of his hand grasping hers. Suddenly, a bulky object loomed ahead of them, and she felt afraid when she recognised it as a light plane. She tightened her grip on Kirk's hand in an effort to hold him back, but he tugged free and began walking towards the plane.

'No, please don't go!' she begged. He kept walking until he reached the plane and swung himself up into the cockpit. As she watched helplessly, he waved to her, then gunned the engines. She put her hands over her ears to shut out the sound and backed away. In a dream, anything is possible, so she felt no surprise when the plane rose vertically from the sand and spiralled upwards into the cloudless sky. Higher and higher, it rose until it vanished completely from her sight.

'Come back, Kirk—oh, please come back!' she screamed, and kept on screaming until she felt a hand shaking her shoulder.

She surfaced unwillingly, not sure for a moment where she was. A light shone overhead and bending over her was Kirk, his expression anxious. 'Kirk,' she smiled, 'it is you!'

'It's Don, anyway,' he said, not unkindly. 'You were having some kind of nightmare.'

Her limbs felt cramped and sore from sleeping in the armchair and she groaned as she stretched full length. 'I didn't mean to wake you. What time is it?'

'It's two in the morning, and I'm glad you woke me. You silly fool, what do you mean trying to sleep like this?'

'I didn't have a choice,' she said with a glint of mischief in her eyes. 'There was a man in my bed.'

'You told me you had a spare folding bed,' he reminded her sternly.

She looked suitably downcast. 'So you remember that? I was hoping you were too ill to notice. Are you feeling all right now?'

He wagged a finger at her. 'Don't try to change the subject, although since you ask—I'm as fit as a fiddle now. These attacks are murder while they last but, fortunately, that isn't usually very long.'

He reached for his clothes draped over the armchair and she sat up. 'What are you doing?'

'I'm going to get dressed and drive home so you can have your bed back—what else?'

She didn't want him to go but couldn't think of anything which would make him stay. 'At least let me make you some coffee before you go.'

'You should really be getting some rest, but—O.K.,' he gave in. As she stood up to go to the kitchen, her foot caught in the hem of her robe and she stumbled, forcing him to catch her to prevent her from falling. As he reached for her, the tie of her robe fell open. She hadn't bothered to put anything on under the garment after her shower and now she stood before him, naked, with the gown swinging around her shoulders and hips.

He surveyed her slim contours for a second, then gave a low groan. 'Oh, Erin, what are you doing to me?' Then he pulled her against him so her body was moulded to his and she could feel the first stirrings of his need for her. His underpants were styled like swimming trunks and moulded every contour of his sinewed body. His coarse mat of chest hair rubbed against her tender skin as he embraced her. Hungrily, he kissed the sides of her neck and the hollow of her throat where her pulse beat wildly in time to the pounding of his heart against her breasts.

She wasn't sure when they passed what Kirk, as a pilot, had called 'the point of no return'. From him, she had learned that it was the point when a plane had reached its half-way point. Unless the pilot turned around then, there would not be enough fuel to go back.

They had reached that point now, she knew, and she also knew with absolute certainty that she did not want to go back, even had it been possible.

'Yes, my darling, yes!' she breathed as he began to lead her towards the bed. With a curse of impatience, he swept her up into his arms and carried her the remaining few feet, to set her gently in the hollow where his body had lain only moments before.

'Are you sure this is what you want?' he asked hoarsely.

'I'm sure,' she confirmed. With that, he stretched full length beside her and opened her robe so it fell away, allowing him an uninterrupted view of her. With slow, firm strokes he began to caress her, moulding her full breasts with his hands, then moving on to her stomach and thighs. The tension inside her mounted to almost unbearable heights. 'Please,' she implored when she could stand it no longer, 'love me, my darling.'

She had been careful not to use his name and risk

destroying the magic of this moment. For now, he was hers again and Leila Coventry might have ceased to exist. Surely now he must remember what they had been to each other?

The moment was as satisfying as she had always known it would be during the years she had been searching for him. 'This is right, so right,' her body cried out as he made love to her. She wished the moment could last for ever.

But it couldn't, no matter how hard she wished it. He took her to all the heights she had imagined during her long search, then brought her gently down again until she lay beside him, trembling with the force of the emotions he had aroused in her.

They hadn't turned out the light and she lay for a long time, watching him as he slept beside her, his face reflecting a peace she hadn't seen there since before he disappeared. He might reproach himself for this in the morning, if he still didn't remember Erin, but for now, some inner part of him knew they belonged together like this.

Contentedly, she curled close against him and drifted off to sleep, feeling at peace herself for the first time in three long years.

This time there were no nightmares to haunt her sleep, so she slept soundly and well, only waking when the sparkling rays of the morning sun glinted into her eyes.

She sat up and rubbed the sleep from her eyes, then looked fondly at the place beside her, feeling a jolt as she saw that the bed was empty. 'Kirk?' she called, wondering if he was in the bathroom. But she couldn't hear any water running and when she ventured inside, he wasn't there either. He must have dressed and left without waking her.

She felt drained. She had known it couldn't last, but she had been so sure that, after last night, he would remember *something*. Desolately, she wandered into the kitchen and put the kettle on to the stove, only then noticing the letter propped against her coffee canister. With shaking fingers, she opened it.

'Dear Erin,' it began, 'First I want to say how sorry I am about last night.'

Tears misted her eyes. Dear God, he had given her the greatest gift she could have desired and he was *sorry*!

'I was thinking only of myself,' he went on, 'and I can only hope that by selfishly giving in to my own desires, I haven't done you any lasting harm. I am writing this now because I feel if we are to work together at all in future after this, we must avoid any repetition of last night. If you want to find another job, I shall understand and will do everything I can to make it easy for you, and ensure that you do not suffer financially because of me. You are right when you say there is something between us. I wish with all my heart that it could be because of a shared past, but I know better than to hope that it could be so.

'I have not reminded you that I am married—we both knew that when we let last night happen, and I will forever reproach myself for not being strong enough to prevent you being hurt. We must not add a third casualty to the list—and of course, I mean Leila.

'I don't ask for your forgiveness because I have done nothing to deserve it, but I do ask for your forbearance.

'Don.'

Angrily, Erin screwed the note into a tight wad and hurled it against the wall. She had known his conscience would suffer because he had made love to her last night, but she didn't deserve to be made to feel cheap like this. They had done nothing wrong and she was not going to be made to feel ashamed, she vowed. He thought the chemistry between them was

nothing more than a sexual attraction which he wasn't
strong enough to resist. But what sort of role did that
cast her in?

The kettle whistled shrilly, and mechanically she
switched it off and made herself a cup of coffee. The
liquid seared her throat, making her choke, and she
got up to pour some milk into the steaming brew.
Sipping the drink made her feel gradually calmer, but
she still wasn't sure what she should do next.

Kirk would understand if she felt she should get
another job, he had written. Maybe that was what she
should do. Get out of his life for ever before she
destroyed them both. And yet, that would be an
admission of defeat and she wasn't yet ready for that.
His choice of wine for their dinner last night and his
unwilling response to what had been their favourite
piece of music proved that he could be reached on an
emotional, if not an intellectual level.

She had been alarmed at the pain he had suffered
when he tried to remember—she hadn't counted on
anything like that. But he had told her the pain would
go once he was able to remember, so perhaps she
would be helping him. But what chance was she going
to have to reach him if he insisted on keeping their
contacts on a purely businesslike level, as he had
implied in his note?

With a deep sigh, she went into the bathroom and
began her morning toilette. The room was still steamy
from Kirk's shower and there was a hint of male odour
in the moisture-laden air. She stood for a moment
with her eyes closed, picturing him here, his lean, hard
body white with soap while water sluiced down on
him from the shower so it ran in rivulets like rain off a
statue of David.

More than ever, she wished she had someone she
could turn to for advice and comfort. Her family was
so far away in England and her limited means made a

visit out of the question. Besides which, her parents believed Kirk was dead and had urged her to accept it too. She had tried to make them understand her feelings without success, until gradually, the letters and phone calls became fewer. Nowadays, they had little contact beyond birthday and Christmas cards. Kirk had no family in Australia either, and since his job involved such erratic hours and long spells away from home, they hadn't made many friends. If she was honest with herself, they could have had a social life— other pilots' families managed it—but they had been so wrapped up in each other they had felt no need for anyone else.

A shudder shook her slender frame. She was starting to think of Kirk as lost to her, she thought with a jolt. She hadn't done that once during the last three years, even when everyone else believed he was dead. Angry with herself for weakening now, she shed her robe and stepped into the shower, turning the water on hard so it shocked her into alertness.

With her skin tingling, she dried herself and got ready to go to work. She hadn't allowed herself to admit defeat in all the time she had been searching for Kirk. She wasn't about to start now, just when she had found him.

CHAPTER FIVE

THE door leading to Kirk's private office was closed when she arrived at work, indicating that he was in conference and did not wish to be disturbed. Well, that was fine with her! She was still seething over his letter—the more she thought about it, the more sordid his note made last night sound. And it hadn't been like that at all, at least not in her eyes.

Angrily, she slapped a file down hard on the desk. How was she ever going to get through to him in his present frame of mind? She couldn't really blame him for his loyalty to Leila since he believed she was his wife, but knowing the truth made Erin writhe inwardly with frustration. He had said Leila had shown him a marriage certificate. It had to be a forgery. If Erin could only get a close look at it! She could, of course, obtain a copy of her own marriage certificate, the original of which had been destroyed in the fire, but that wouldn't make Kirk believe that he was the man named on the certificate. No, she had to make him understand that Leila's so-called evidence was fraudulent. But how? The only way she could think of was if Kirk himself remembered the truth.

The puzzle gnawed at her as she tried to concentrate on the work awaiting her on her desk. Kirk must have left her flat very early to be able to dictate all the letters she found on the dictaphone, unless he had done them in the car on the way to work. She was glad she was blessed with a faster-than-average typing speed so she could get through them all in reasonable time.

At mid-morning, she was interrupted by a buzz

from her intercom. Frowning, because she had already
been interrupted innumerable times by the telephone,
she flicked the switch. 'Yes, Mr Sands,' she said
formally, unable to keep the chill out of her voice. He
had said he wanted a purely business relationship. See
how he liked it when he got it!

'Would you have morning coffee for two sent in,
please, Erin?'

'Of course, Mr Sands, right away.' She snapped the
switch off quickly before he could comment on her
new attitude, then dialled the canteen's extension and
ordered a tray for him.

When it arrived, she debated whether to send the
girl from the canteen in with it, but she was dressed in
an overall a size too large and her hair was untidily
pinned up—not at all the sort of image Kirk would
want to present to his visitor. With a sigh, Erin took
the tray from the girl and knocked on Kirk's door.

'Come in,' he responded, and she pushed the door
open with one hand, then braced it open with her hip
while she manoeuvred the tray around it.

'Here, let me help you with that,' Kirk's visitor said
when he caught sight of her, and jumped up to help.

'Hello, Mr Burrows,' she smiled, recognising him.
She set the tray down on the low table between the
two men. 'How do you prefer your coffee?'

'The way I like my women—hot and strong,' he
teased. 'Er . . . no offence, ma'am.'

'None taken,' she assured him, and looked pointedly
at Kirk, who was frowning blackly. 'We are all grown-
ups, after all.'

John Burrows looked as though he would like to add a
further comment to this, but Kirk quickly intervened.
'We can serve ourselves, thanks, Erin. That will be all.'

She resisted an insane urge to drop him a mocking
curtsey as she said, 'Yes, Mr Sands.' But her eyes
were flashing as she made a demure and proper exit.

With the door firmly closed between them, she vented her rage on the filing cabinet by thumping it hard with her fist. All she succeeded in doing was bruising her hand, which she nursed self-pityingly. Damn Kirk Wilding—Don Sands, or whoever he was! Who did he think he was, treating her like this? He wouldn't admit that he wanted Erin for himself, and yet he had been jealous of John Burrows for admiring her so openly. She had a good mind to go out with Burrows if he asked her again, just to show Kirk he couldn't have everything his own way!

Then she saw how unreasonable she was behaving. Kirk couldn't help the way he was reacting. As long as he believed he was married to Leila, he wouldn't dare admit his feelings towards Erin, even to himself. His sense of decency was much too strong for that, and wasn't that one of the very qualities she loved about him?

Still, the idea of letting John Burrows take her out had merit, she mused, sipping her own cup of coffee contemplatively. However forward his remarks had been, he struck her as being a window-shopper when it came to women. Not that her experience of men was so vast, she smiled to herself, remembering how shy she had been before she met Kirk. But she had grown up a great deal since then and she was sure that, without encouragement from her, John Burrows would remain the perfect gentleman, so going out with him wouldn't entail any of the risks she had taken with Bert Halstead. At the distasteful memory of Halstead's treatment of her, she began to wonder where he had disappeared to. She hadn't seen him since the night of the Ball, so perhaps he was away on leave. His absence didn't worry her—the opposite, in fact, but she had the uneasy feeling that he would want to settle his score with her sooner or later.

Anxious to dismiss all thoughts of Halstead from her

mind, she drained her cup and set to finishing the letters ready for Kirk's signature when the meeting was over. They all concerned aspects of the coming merger and, when added to the details she had already assimilated from the file, she began to feel that she had a good grasp of the transaction—enough, in fact, to make a few minor improvements to the language in the letters. With luck, Kirk would not object, if he even noticed her contribution.

It was almost one o'clock by the time Kirk's office door opened and John Burrows appeared. 'You must have thought we were in there for the duration,' he smiled at her, stretching to ease his cramped muscles.

He was quite a good-looking man, Erin thought, watching him. He was half a head shorter than Kirk and his build was slimmer and more boyish, but his ready smile and warm manner more than made up for any physical shortcomings. She found herself returning his smile effortlessly. 'Your hotel relayed this message for you,' she told him, handing him the note she had made.

He glanced at it, then back to her. 'Nothing that won't keep, thanks. So there's nothing to stop you and me having lunch together if you would do me the honour?'

Her glance went quickly to Kirk's door. 'Thank you, Mr Burrows, but . . .'

'It's John, please. There's no need to worry about Don. I distinctly heard him say he's waiting for an international phone call, so he's having a sandwich in his office.'

'Oh, I see.' There didn't seem to be anything else she could do but agree. She was still simmering over Kirk's apology which had made their night together seem underhanded instead of the beautiful moment she cherished, so it was probably better if she didn't stay in the office for lunch. She might be tempted to give Kirk a piece of her mind. 'All right John, I'll be happy to join you.'

'That's the girl! I'll just square things with your boss so he won't mind if you're away a little longer than usual.'

Before she could say that this thought might not be appreciated by Kirk and, in any case, they could easily fit lunch into her allotted hour, John had disappeared back into Kirk's office. A minute later he returned looking pleased with himself. 'He says to take all the time we want,' he assured her.

If it had been anyone but John Burrows doing the asking, Erin was certain Kirk wouldn't have said any such thing, but she merely nodded agreement and picked up the sheaf of telephone messages which had accumulated for Kirk while he was in conference.

He was bent over some paperwork when she timidly approached his desk. 'Your messages,' she offered, placing them to one side of his desk.

He barely acknowledged her presence, as she started out of the room, but he looked up as she reached the door, and she was startled to see an expression of cold disapproval on his face. 'Don't be too long. I'll need you to type these conference notes for me this afternoon,' he said in a surly tone.

Erin could hardly believe her ears. He was jealous because she had agreed to have lunch with John Burrows! Her heart sang at the very idea, since it meant he did have some strong feelings towards her. She longed to reassure him that there was no one else in the whole world for her but him. Such an admission would get her nowhere, however, while there was a good chance that inflaming his jealousy might have an effect on his memory. 'I'll make sure John gets me back in plenty of time,' she said with deliberate lightness, feeling a pang of guilt when she saw how thunderous her comment made him look.

Before she could give herself the chance to take it back, she escaped from his office. His unhappy expression haunted her as she and John Burrows drove to a restaurant John said Kirk had recommended to him some time before.

He was taking her to Marcel's, she discovered with a start. It was the same restaurant Kirk had intended to take her to the previous night, when she had suggested they go to her flat instead. Since she couldn't tell John that she would prefer to go somewhere else without giving him an explanation, she made herself look pleased and followed him into the restaurant.

By day it was sunny and colourful, in contrast to the smoky moodiness of the previous night. She was glad that a stranger led them to a table for two set in a bay window. Marcel might have made some comment about Erin and Kirk leaving before he could accommodate them last night, and that would only arouse John's curiosity further regarding the nature of her relationship with his future partner.

'This is mighty nice,' John enthused, as he surveyed the extensive menu. 'Good atmosphere, too, although I'd still like to track down a place with real Aussie cuisine.'

'About all I can suggest is kangaroo-tail soup and hot damper—bushman's bread,' she laughed. 'We don't really have a cooking style of our own.'

'Then I'll make sure I try some of that soup before I go home to the States.' Since there was none on the menu today, they laughingly settled for medaillons of veal wrapped in bacon and served with fresh pasta topped with a raw tomato sauce. Although she swore she wouldn't be able to eat desert after that, John talked her into a zesty-sounding treat of orange cream decorated with spearmint leaves.

Between courses, they talked about the coming merger between John Burrows' American company and the Coventry Corporation, of which Sands Engineering was part. John raised an eyebrow at the extent of Erin's knowledge of the transaction, then settled into a detailed discussion on some of the finer points of the deal.

By the time their dessert was served, they were arguing amicably over whether the U.S. or Australia offered the best centre of operations. Each had his own beliefs and reasons, and Erin found herself enjoying the debate immensely.

'You're really quite a business woman,' John told her admiringly. 'You know, if Sands won't bring you over to the States with him, I've a mind to invite you over myself. British secretaries are in big demand back home.'

'But I'm not British,' she demurred. 'I was born in Australia.'

He looked surprised. 'Really? From your accent I would have taken you for English.'

'That's because I spent most of my teenage years there. My father is the overseas representative for one of our large retailers here, and he's permanently based in Britain.'

'Then you're all alone here?'

At his sympathetic tone, she was annoyed to find a tear filming her eye and she blinked it away, but not before he had caught the movement. 'You *are* lonely, aren't you? No relatives here?'

She sighed. 'Not a one. Both my parents come from small families. But I wasn't lonely until three years ago.'

'Was that when you divorced your husband?' he asked gently. She realised he had reached his own conclusion after hearing her called 'Mrs' Wilding.

'Divorced? Oh, no.' She went on to tell him about Kirk's disappearance and her long, painful search for him when she alone believed that he was still alive.

What would he say, she wondered, if he found out that her missing husband was the man he knew as Don Sands? There was no way he could make the connection from her tale, she knew, so she wasn't betraying Kirk by telling John her story. And it was heavenly to be able to pour her heart out to someone, she realised now. She hadn't been fully aware of just how much she had needed a shoulder to cry on.

'What makes you so sure he's still alive?' John asked quietly.

'Because I've seen him, touched him, been with him,' she longed to cry out. But instead, she said, 'I just know, that's all.'

He covered her hand with his own in a friendly gesture. 'I admire your loyalty, Erin. I hope you hear some news of your husband real soon.'

She nodded, too overcome by her own emotions to speak. Then she glanced at her watch and gave a start when she saw how late it was. 'I'll have to get back,' she said regretfully. She had enjoyed talking to him and told him so.

He grinned ruefully. 'Your gratitude wasn't really what I had in mind when I asked you out to lunch,' he began, and raised a warning hand when she began to interrupt. 'It's all right, honey. I'm glad we had this chance to talk. It made me see what a poor second I would have come behind this Kirk of yours.'

Miserably, she traced a pattern on the tablecloth with her finger. 'I'm sorry, John.'

'Don't be. At least I know where I stand. Shall we go?' In silence, he escorted her out of the restaurant and back to his car for the short drive back to the factory.

'I'll just drop you at the entrance, if that's okay?'

'Aren't you coming in?' she queried nervously. Somehow she didn't like the idea of facing Kirk alone after his bleak reaction to her announcement that she was lunching with John Burrows.

'Not this time. I have another meeting across town this afternoon.'

At the main entrance, she started to get out of the car and he laid a hand on her forearm. 'There's just one thing I don't understand, Erin.'

'What's that?' she asked, puzzled.

'Oh, I understand about your husband and all. But where does Don Sands fit into your plans?'

'Don Sands?' She stared at him for a moment before making the mental connection. 'Oh ... he's ... he's my boss, of course. Why do you ask?'

He seemed to be choosing his words with great care. 'Well, it's just ... hell, my company's old-fashioned, that's all. And it seems to me, husband or no, there's something between you and Don.'

'Would it make any difference to the merger if there was?' she asked tensely.

He sighed. 'Maybe, and maybe not. I just like to know the kind of man I'm dealing with, that's all. I know he's married ...'

'... and so am I,' she finished heavily. She should have known his questions during lunch had been leading somewhere. It wasn't only that he was interested in her for herself, after all. He was mainly anxious to ensure she didn't contaminate his precious business deal with her dubious morals! Before she could say something she would regret, she slammed the car door shut and started to walk away. Behind her, she heard him wind down the window.

'Erin, wait a second ...'

She kept walking, biting her lip to hold back her tears. So that was how her actions appeared to an outsider, was it? As if she didn't care about her own married state and had no scruples about chasing after someone else's husband, either. Dear lord, was that how Kirk perceived her, too? What was she supposed to do? She couldn't just walk away from Kirk and pretend he didn't exist, yet how much more of this nightmare situation could she take?

In the sanctuary of the ladies' room, she stared at herself in the mirror. She hardly recognised the white-faced waif who stared back at her. Because of the amount of time she had spent indoors over the last few weeks she had lost her healthy tan, and the strain of seeing Kirk every day, knowing he was her husband even though he didn't recognise her, had also taken a toll. Without much enthusiasm, she made what improvements she could with make-up and a comb, then braced herself to face Kirk again.

He was pacing up and down the outer office when she walked in, and glanced pointedly at his watch.

'I know I'm late,' she said tiredly. 'But John . . . Mr Burrows did ask your permission.'

'You mean he told me he was taking you to lunch,' he amended gruffly. 'I warned you that I wanted some conference notes typed this afternoon.'

'And I said I would do them. Even if I have to stay here all night.'

She followed him into his office and stood silently by his desk while he sorted through a stack of papers for the ones he wanted her to type. At last he handed her a sheaf of them, but made no move to relinquish them when she reached out. 'Erin . . .' he began.

'Yes?' she responded dully, not looking at him.

'What did you and John Burrows do while you were together?'

She had a childish impulse to tell him that John had taken her to a hotel room, thrown her on the bed, removed all her clothes and made violent love to her. Would that get the reaction she wanted from Kirk—or would it merely reinforce his already dim view of her character? 'We had lunch, that's all,' she said instead.

'That's all? Come on, Erin, you don't expect me to believe that after last night at your flat . . .'

She could feel angry red colour staining her cheeks at what he was inferring. 'You bastard!' she hissed with all the fury she could muster. 'Your conscience is bothering you because you slept with me last night and you're trying to pin all the blame on me, aren't you?'

'No, I'm not . . . all right, I am,' he admitted. 'God, Erin, you can't imagine how badly I feel about last night. I had no right to make love to you, no matter what I felt.'

'What did you feel?' she demanded.

'What difference does it make now?'

'Everything—to me.'

He looked down at his desk as if he was looking through it to his own soul. 'All right, if you must know, I think I could be falling in love with you. I don't know how else to explain the way I feel when you're around.'

She leaned across the desk and gripped both his arms with her hands. 'Don't think of it like that. You have to believe me—what you feel for me is right. Some part of you remembers me . . . remembers that you love me.' Her voice broke on a sob and he looked at her strangely.

'Oh, Erin, if only it was that simple! When you talk like this you almost have me believing it could be true.'

'It *is* true,' she swore. 'You've got to stop closing your mind to that possibility.'

Kirk sat down at his desk and buried his head in both hands. 'Yes, I am closing my mind,' he conceded. 'But you must understand, it's been the only way I could have stayed sane during the last three years.'

'But I'm here now, to help you—if you'll let me,' she said to herself. She hardly dared to believe that at last she might be making some progress. If she could only convince him not to dismiss her story out of hand . . . that was the first vital step. 'Then you admit I might possibly be telling the truth?' she asked carefully.

He looked up at her with pain-filled eyes. 'If I admit even that much, I shake the very foundations of my existence. You're asking a lot.'

'I'm only asking you to open your mind. Won't you do that much for me?' She held her breath as she waited for his answer and the seconds stretched into the longest minutes she had ever known. Suddenly the tension was shattered by the shrilling of the telephone on his desk. Automatically, she reached for it. 'Mr Sands' office?'

'May I speak to him urgently, please? I'm calling from Cowra Hospital.'

Cowra? Erin was sure that was the district west of the Blue Mountains where Leila's brother had his sheep station. Erin's heart began to beat faster. Maybe something had happened to Leila's sister-in-law—Erin recalled Kirk mentioning something about the woman recovering from an operation, which was why Leila had flown up there in the first place. She handed the receiver to Kirk and explained who was calling, then waited anxiously as he took the call.

His face became white and his expression grew intense as he listened, and he gripped the receiver with fierce intensity. 'When did this happen? No, I've been in conference all morning.' The look he gave Erin was filled with agony. 'Yes, I was . . . out . . . last night as well. Of course, I'll come at once. Thank you. Goodbye.'

Like a man in a dream, he replaced the receiver and stared at Erin in horror.

'What is it? What's happened?' she asked, afraid that she had already guessed the answer.

'It's Leila,' he explained, confirming her worst fears. 'She was out riding on her brother's property and her horse stumbled on a rabbit hole. She took a very bad fall.'

'How is she?'

'She's paralysed from the waist down,' he said hopelessly.

Erin's mind went numb. She had no love at all for the heiress who had stolen Kirk from her, but the thought of anyone so young and vital being crippled horrified her. 'When did it happen?' she asked.

'Yesterday. They tell me she was returning from an all-day ride. They tried to call me at home last night, but . . .'

'You couldn't have known this would happen,' she said desperately, sensing what he was thinking. 'Why didn't they call you again this morning?'

'They tried, it seems. Or at least, Leila's brother did.'

What was he suggesting? 'Oh no, you can't think that I deliberately withheld a message?' she demanded.

He ran a hand through his hair, tousling it, then rested his chin on one hand. 'No, of course I don't think any such thing. I left instructions that I wasn't to be disturbed, remember?'

The pile of telephone messages she had delivered to him before she went to lunch still lay untouched on his desk. He riffled through them and pulled out two from a Mr Tom Coventry.

'Leila's brother?' she asked.

He nodded. 'It wouldn't have meant very much to you, except as one of the corporation's directors.'

'But he did ask to be called back urgently.'

Kirk smiled thinly and gestured at the pile of messages. 'How many of them say that?'

Erin understood what he meant. 'All but one of them.'

'So you see, there's no one to blame. It was just bad luck that the message took so long getting through— not that it would have made any difference anyway.'

Still, she couldn't rid herself of the dreadful feeling that he held her responsible for what had happened. Not directly, of course, but as a kind of penance because he had been making love to her at the very moment the hospital had been trying to reach him. 'What are you going to do now?' she asked.

'I'll fly to Cowra in the company jet and bring Leila back to Sydney with me as soon as she's fit to travel.' He gave her instructions for how to organise the jet for him and asked her to arrange a hire car to meet him at Cowra, and she hurried back to her own office to set things in motion. While she managed to appear outwardly calm, inside she felt sick with misery. She had been so close to a breakthrough with Kirk, she was sure. Now he would have to give all his attention to Leila, who certainly needed him. But while Erin felt sorry for Leila's tragic condition, part of her was unable to stop hating the heiress. Even though she was ashamed of her own reaction, Erin couldn't break free of the nagging fear that if Leila was indeed paralysed beyond hope of recovery, there would be no way for Kirk to leave her, even if he did recover his memory.

Kirk owed Leila a substantial debt of gratitude, Erin knew. Leila had been the one to rescue him after his plane crashed into the sea, Erin was convinced now, and Leila had also stuck by him when others tried to take advantage of his amnesia for their own gain.

Now, the tables were turned and Leila needed him. His personal code of honour would never let him desert her under such circumstances, no matter what it cost him—or Erin.

The two weeks that followed were a nightmare for Erin. On her shoulders fell the full weight of the paperwork affecting the merger. She was constantly called on to arrange the transfer of documents back and forth between Cowra and Sydney for Kirk's signature. The thought of him at Leila's bedside tortured Erin, although she couldn't fault his reasoning. By his own beliefs, he was doing the only thing he could.

She compensated for her inner turmoil by working like a woman demented, leaving no task undone.

'You're a marvel, you know that?' John Burrows told her as he surveyed some documents she had just typed for his approval. He hadn't referred to her relationship with Kirk since the stormy after-lunch scene two weeks ago, and she assumed he was pleased to see Kirk acting the dutiful husband—and no doubt pleased about the distance the accident had put between Kirk and Erin. John had expressed his regrets at Leila's tragedy, but Erin suspected he saw it as a blessing in disguise for Kirk's marriage. So there was no reason now why John couldn't be pleasant to Erin again.

For her part, she was too weary of spirit to defend herself. 'I'm just doing my job,' she said quietly in response to his praise.

'And a first-class one it is,' he beamed. 'I don't know of anyone else who could have taken this office over at such a crucial time, and coped as well as you've done under very trying circumstances.'

'Thank you,' she said politely, wondering to herself what else she could have done. She knew how much the business meant to Kirk and she couldn't just walk out on him now when he needed help. There was also her own pressing need for a job, but that had been the least of her considerations. Kirk was right about one thing—with her qualifications, she wouldn't have been unemployed for long.

Keeping busy also ensured she could stay out of the way of Bert Halstead, who had returned from his leave soon after Kirk flew to Cowra. He had raised a cynical eyebrow when he discovered Erin had been instated as Kirk's personal assistant and sneeringly suggested that her dancing with Kirk at the Spring Ball had been calculated to achieve just this result.

'I can assure you the Ball has nothing to do with my promotion, Mr Halstead,' she told him icily.

'So it's "Mr Halstead" now, is it? Too good for me, these days? Or have I served my purpose in your little scheme of things?'

It was so uncomfortably close to the truth that Erin couldn't help blushing. She *had* used the personnel manager, manoeuvring him into taking her to the Ball so she could be near Kirk, but he would never understand her motives. 'Think what you like, I can't stop you,' she said tiredly.

'That's true, you can't stop me,' he agreed, and a tremor passed through her as she absorbed the double meaning in his statement. She had been expecting more trouble from him, but she had been hoping it could be avoided. She resolved to stay well out of Halstead's way as much as possible, especially while Kirk was away.

With the amount of work she had to do, this wasn't too difficult to achieve. She was already coming in much earlier than the other secretaries in order to keep up with everything.

It was on one such session that she heard a movement in the outer office. She had decided to work at Kirk's desk, partly for convenience—he had all the reference materials she needed there—and partly from the reassuring sense of his nearness she gained from sitting here in his chair. She froze. 'Who's there?' she called.

The door swung wide and she hardly recognised the man standing framed in the opening. He looked haggard and worn, years older than when she had last seen him just over a fortnight ago. 'Kirk!' she breathed. 'How are you?'

'How do I look?' he asked in a wry tone.

'Terrible,' she said flatly, taking in his shadowed eyes and the obvious fact that he hadn't shaved for some time.

'That's exactly how I feel,' he groaned, and lowered himself into one of the visitor's chairs.

At once, Erin realised she was still sitting in his chair and quickly got up to join him on the other side of the desk. 'Can I get you anything?'

'I know it's early, but a drink would be useful,' he said, passing a hand over his eyes as if the fluorescent light hurt them.

At once she went to the bar in the corner and without asking for his preference, poured him a double Scotch with a splash of iced water.

When she handed it to him, he drank half of it in one swallow, then set the glass unsteadily on the coffee table between them. 'I hear you've been coping magnificently here. The Americans are really singing your praises.'

'I'm glad they're happy,' she said tensely. She longed to throw herself at him and gather him into her arms, pressing his head against her breast so she could stroke the tousled hair like a child's. 'How is Leila?' she asked with difficulty.

He took another swallow of his drink before he answered. 'As far as the doctors are concerned, she's perfectly healthy.' Hope flared briefly in Erin's breast, only to be dashed again as he went on, 'Except that she's still paralysed.'

Erin was baffled. 'But if there's nothing wrong with her, then why . . .'

'. . . why can't she walk?' he finished for her. 'That's what we would all like to know, including Leila herself. The fact is, there's no medical reason for it, but she's lost the use of her legs.'

'Psychosomatic,' murmured Erin.

'That's right. A physical symptom which most likely has an emotional origin,' he agreed. 'At least, that's what her doctors say. But she's just as paralysed as if there's a medical reason.'

With a flash of insight, Erin understood the reason for Leila's paralysis, even if no one else did. The heiress knew she was in danger of losing Kirk, so her mind had found a way of hanging on to him. As long as she was physically dependent on him, he wouldn't be able to leave her, even if he did regain his memory. Erin knew it was useless to try to explain all this to Kirk. He would simply refuse to believe that Leila could be so devious. And he would argue that Leila's paralysis was real—which it undoubtedly was. Erin was well aware of the mind's power over the body. Hadn't her own willpower sustained her for the last three years?

In a way, she felt a strange kinship with Leila. They were both fighting for the same end. But Erin had a sick feeling that Leila was by far the most ruthless.

CHAPTER SIX

KIRK sat in his office looking so weary that Erin's heart went out to him, but she could think of nothing she could do or say to comfort him. 'Have you thought any more about . . . us?' she asked in a frightened whisper.

He stared at her in undisguised despair. 'I've thought about almost nothing else,' he confessed, 'especially about where I was and what I was doing the day Leila got hurt.'

Her cry came from the heart. 'Surely you can't be blaming yourself for that? Nothing you could have done would have changed what happened.'

He massaged his eyes with one hand. 'Maybe not. But at least I wouldn't be feeling so damned guilty now.'

She jumped to her feet in a rush of angry reaction. 'Guilty? You make it sound so . . . so sordid!'

'Well, wasn't it?' he demanded harshly.

Erin could hardly credit what she was hearing. 'No!' she denied vehemently. 'Can't you look at it from my side just once? You *are* my husband, even though you can't remember our relationship, so there's nothing for you to feel guilty about.'

'Stop it!' he commanded in such a fierce tone that she jumped. 'I'm sorry,' he relented, 'I know this must be hard for you, epecially if there's any truth in what you tell me.'

'If?' she interrupted angrily. 'I've told you . . .'

'Let me finish,' he insisted. 'What I'm trying to say is that the truth is no longer what's important.'

She turned tear-filled eyes to him. 'Then what is?'

'A woman in a wheelchair, who needs me. She was there when I needed help, so I can't let her down now when the tables are turned.'

This is what Erin had dreaded ever since she heard the news of Leila's accident. 'You can help her without turning your back on the past,' she suggested, but with an edge of hopelessness in her voice.

'How? By deserting her? No, Erin, that's not the way it's going to be. Besides which, the only past I have is what you tell me existed between us, so, for me, there's nothing to turn my back on.' He reached for her hand and she was achingly aware of the fiery touch of his skin against hers. 'Please try to understand.'

She tried to pull free, but he gripped her hand more tightly, turning her so she was forced to face him and endure the beseeching gaze he directed at her. 'I'm no saint. You're asking too much,' she breathed.

A sigh of despair hissed out from between his clenched teeth. 'I have to ask a lot more,' he told her softly. 'I want you to come to Eaglewood and work there with me so I can be close to Leila in case she needs me.'

The room whirled around Erin and for a moment she feared she was going to faint. 'You can't be serious?'

'I'm afraid I am. The doctors are worried that depression brought on by her paralysis has made her suicidal. Someone has to be on call all the time.'

'But surely, one of the servants . . .'

'I'm the only one she'll talk to. She's sedated now, which is how I was able to get away to come here, but in her present state of mind I daren't leave her side for very long.'

Erin sank down on to the chair opposite Kirk and stared at him blankly. The idea of working under Leila's own roof was beyond bearing. 'You'll have to get one of the other secretaries,' she said flatly.

He shook his head. 'One of the others won't do. You've made too big an impact with our American friends. They insist that you continue to work on the merger as a condition of the deal going through.'

A hysterical laugh bubbled up inside her. She had been too efficient for her own good, and now she was to be punished by being forced to work alongside her husband while he lived with another woman under her very eyes. 'You could always walk away,' a traitorous voice inside her suggested—but that would mean giving Kirk up for good, and she wasn't prepared to face that yet.

Another puzzling thought occurred to her. 'But won't Leila's accident prevent the merger going ahead anyway?'

He frowned impatiently. 'There's still a month until the contracted date, and Leila's paralysis may right itself by then. Her doctors feel the excitement of the merger may be just what she needs to snap her out of her depression and speed her recovery—which is another reason for moving the office out to Eaglewood, where she can be involved if she wants to.'

Erin forced her voice to sound steady even though every nerve ending in her body quivered with nervous anticipation. 'Very well, I'll come,' she conceded.

For a brief moment, his iron control slipped and the full extent of his gratitude shone in his eyes, warming her in its tender glow. 'Thank you,' he said simply, then more briskly, 'we'll take what we need from here for now. The rest can be picked up by courier as we need it. Then I'll drive you to your flat to pick up your things.'

'My—my things?' she asked stupidly. 'What do you mean?'

'If you're going to stay at Eaglewood you'll need some changes of clothes, toiletries and so on.'

'Stay at Eaglewood?' she echoed, knowing she

sounded foolish but unable to absorb what he was saying.

Kirk sighed impatiently. 'I thought that's what we just agreed.'

'You said work there,' she corrected him. 'I don't know if I could actually live there.'

'I'm sorry if I didn't make that clear,' he said not unkindly, 'but as I explained, Leila needs me on call at all hours. I won't know what hours will be available for working, so it would be best if you were also on call. Please don't say you're letting me down now.'

'No, I wouldn't do that,' she said carefully. Her mind was racing ahead to the nerve-racking prospect of sharing a house with the woman who had stolen her husband, perhaps sleeping in an adjoining room while they . . . while they . . . her mind refused to accept that they could actually make love while she was living under their roof. Then she remembered Leila's condition and felt a hot flush of shame spreading through her body. She was actually glad that Leila was physically incapacitated because it meant she would be unable to share Kirk's bed. Oh God! What sort of person was she turning into, that she could feel this pleased about another person's infirmity?

Kirk glanced at his watch. 'We'd better be on our way before Leila wakes up and finds I've gone.'

Erin deliberately put her mind into neutral to block out any further thoughts about the days ahead of her. If she dwelled on it too much, she would turn around and run as fast as she could in the opposite direction, and that would mean the end of any hope for her and Kirk.

Like an automaton, she helped him to collect the files and materials they would need to continue working away from the office. Then they loaded everything into his Mercedes for the drive to her flat, where she hurriedly piled a selection of clothes into a suitcase. During the last three years she had done so much travelling in her search for Kirk that she could pack swiftly and efficiently, so she soon assembled everything she would need and Kirk helped her carry them down to the car.

'You haven't brought much,' he commented as he placed her luggage in the car.

'Well, this ... this arrangement won't be for very long, surely?' she asked him.

His expression was grim as he slammed the boot lid with more force than was really called for. 'We have no way of knowing. It all depends on Leila.'

Erin settled herself in the passenger seat, and as they drove, she was reminded of her first ride in this car, after he found her waiting for him. He had kissed her then with fierce passion, not because he remembered her but because he thought she was an opportunist and that was the pay-off he believed she wanted. She shuddered involuntarily. He was right, everything depended on Leila—but not in the way he meant. Only when the heiress was well again would Kirk permit himself the luxury of exploring his own feelings. Which meant that Erin's happiness now depended on Leila as well. 'What shall I do about my flat?' she asked.

'If you give me the name of your landlord, I'll see that the company pays your rent for as long as you need to stay at Eaglewood—unless you'd prefer to let the place go, of course.'

'No, I'll keep the flat, thanks.' She wanted to have it there as a kind of bolthole in case she needed it. If Leila never regained the use of her legs, Erin might be glad of the flat as a refuge in future. It would be the only one she had, she told herself grimly.

In spite of her inner trepidation, she looked around curiously as they neared the Coventry family home. Erin had only seen pictures of Eaglewood in home decorator magazines and she was unprepared for the imposing reality.

The mansion was located in an exclusive part of Stokes Point, a peninsula jutting out between the surf and the lazy Pittwater tides. All around the house, nature's zest was abundantly displayed with tall eucalyptus trees and mangroves giving tantalising glimpses of Careel Bay on the left and Pittwater on the right. The house itself nestled among sprays of frangipanis, palms and ferns and through the trees, Erin could see cut into the sandstone, a staircase leading down to what was probably a private beach.

'There are koalas in these trees,' Kirk told her, pointing to a sign warning drivers to look out for koalas crossing the road. 'We get possums on the back verandahs and an occasional spiny anteater in the grounds.'

Erin, a nature lover, would have been delighted by all this if he hadn't prefaced the statement with 'we', reminding her painfully that this was Leila Coventry's domain. The heiress had inherited the property along with the Coventry Corporation, when her father, Henry Coventry, died three years ago, Erin recalled reading at the time.

She drew a deep breath as they rounded a wide driveway and were confronted by Eaglewood in all its grandeur. The house was an unusual combination of Victorian charm and 1920s extravagance. The original single-storeyed sandstone dwelling could be seen on one side, but it was now joined to a Roman villa-style building with a two-storeyed wing completing a U-shape on the other side.

Kirk drew up in a courtyard where sunlight sparkled off a fishpond, surrounded by lush tropical gardens. When they got out of the car, Erin could see that the verandahs running the length of the house still had their original tallowwood floorboards. Altogether, the property was an extraordinary blend of old and new styles and materials, just the sort of place she would have imagined successive generations of the same family would have owned, each generation putting its own stamp on it. Which were Leila's contributions? she wondered with a touch of asperity, then reminded herself that Leila wouldn't have had time to make many changes, since she had only been in charge of Eaglewood for three years.

They entered the house through a portico which was flanked by two old gnarled daphne trees which gave the property its name, and Erin found herself in a hallway which came from yet another architectural era. She waited, unsure of which way to go, until Kirk followed her inside, carrying her luggage.

He rang a bell set into an alcove near the door and Erin jumped as a grey-haired woman in a black dress and floral apron materialised seemingly from nowhere. 'Ethel, this is Mrs Wilding,' Kirk introduced her. 'Erin, our housekeeper, Mrs Niland.'

'How do you do, Mrs Niland,' Erin said nervously. She was unaccustomed to dealing with staff and hoped she wouldn't make a fool of herself in this grand setting.

Ethel Niland immediately set her mind to rest. 'It's so good of you to come here like this,' she said warmly, then at Erin's quizzical glance towards Kirk, she went on, 'Mr Don told me all about why you have to move your office here. It's very kind of you to do this for Miss Leila, seeing as how it must be disrupting your own life.'

She wasn't doing it for 'Miss Leila', Erin thought uncomfortably, but she didn't disillusion the housekeeper, who obviously thought the sun rose and set on the Coventry family. Despite Mrs Niland's claim that Kirk had told her 'all about' the situation, Erin seriously doubted that he would have told the housekeeper anything more than the surface details. If he had, she doubted whether she would be receiving such a warm welcome.

Kirk interrupted her thoughts. 'I'll leave you in Ethel's care for now, Erin, while I look in on Leila.'

As she watched him walk away, Erin felt a stab of pain. How was she ever going to endure this situation? She must have been mad to think that she could live here, even for a short time, constantly being reminded that at present Kirk's allegiance was to another woman.

'This way, dear,' Mrs Niland encouraged her, picking up one of her cases. Since there didn't seem to be anything else she could do, Erin picked up the other bag and followed the housekeeper up the broad, polished wooden staircase.

'Have you worked here long, Mrs Niland?' she asked, more to divert her troubled thoughts than because she wanted information.

'The Coventrys are the only family I've got, dear. I was Mr Henry's housekeeper too,' Ethel said proudly. 'I've lived at Eaglewood since I was a girl of sixteen.'

Since the woman was obviously well into her fifties, Erin could understand that she regarded the mansion as her only home. She was glad Mrs Niland didn't know the real reason she was here. She had a feeling the news would be received very badly.

'What a delightful room,' she said sincerely when she was shown into what she was told was to be her bedroom.

The room was spacious in typical 1920s style, with finishes which complemented its grandeur. The walls were the original coursed sandstone with two multipaned, double hung windows trimmed with louvre shutters, giving on to a spectacular view of the rolling Pittwater surf. In the centre of the room was a substantial oak bedstead covered with a modern continental quilt, although its Liberty print cover had been chosen to harmonise with the room.

'Shall I unpack for you?' the housekeeper asked.

'Oh no, I can manage, thank you—you must have much more pressing duties,' Erin told her. She was anxious to be alone with her thoughts for a while. Everything had happened much too quickly.

Mrs Niland didn't seem to be offended by her refusal. Instead, she seemed flattered by Erin's estimation of her importance. 'Yes, there is a lot to do, and it's hard to get other staff these days,' she confided. She opened a door on to an adjoining room. 'This is your bathroom if you'd like to freshen up. Dinner is at eight.'

'Thank you,' Erin said again. 'Do you ... I mean ... is dinner very formal here?'

'Goodness me, no!' Mrs Niland laughed. 'It used to be in Mr Henry's day, but now, nobody even bothers to dress up. These days, things are kept very simple, especially at present with Miss Leila so ill.'

Erin nodded her acknowledgement and was relieved when Mrs Niland left her alone at last. She made a brief inspection of the spacious bathroom adjoining her bedroom, then unpacked the few clothes she had brought from her flat. They looked very meagre when hung in the huge antique Tasmanian oak wardrobe, but she wasn't here for decoration, so it didn't matter how she was dressed.

By the time she finished her unpacking, there was just time for a soak in the bathtub before she joined Kirk for dinner. The sandwiches they had had sent into the office at lunchtime, while they organised the things they would need to bring to Eaglewood had taken the edge off her appetite so she wasn't very hungry, but she was curious. Would Leila join them for dinner? Probably not, since she was still recovering from her accident. Erin didn't know whether she would be relieved or not if Leila wasn't there. The confrontation between them would have to take place sometime and the sooner it did, the better she would feel. Somehow she doubted whether Kirk had even told Leila that Erin was in the house. It would be an ugly moment when she found out.

Determinedly, Erin pushed such thoughts from her mind and turned the taps on full to fill the deep bathtub with steaming water, liberally lacing it with some rose-scented crystals she found in a jar on the side of the bath. Soon the air was redolent with the fragrance of roses.

Sighing with pleasure, she stepped out of her clothes and slid into the water which closed around her like a lover's arms. If only she could stay in this warm, sweet-scented cocoon for ever! So much had happened during the last few hours that she felt slightly giddy and welcomed this brief respite to sort out her confused thoughts.

Now she was able to think about it properly, she doubted whether the merger could depend on her involvement. Could it be that Kirk wanted her here in the house with him and was only using the business deal as an excuse? It seemed to be the only reasonable explanation. But it would also mean that Kirk had begun to believe her story, or at least give her the benefit of the doubt. He couldn't desert Leila in her present crippled condition, but perhaps he meant to do something about it once Leila showed signs of recovery.

If she recovered, Erin reminded herself. The doctors thought that Leila's paralysis was emotional rather than physical, but it did not make her condition any less real.

Reluctantly, Erin stood up in the bath, letting the rose-scented droplets cascade off her body. Her skin felt sleek and satiny from the oils in the crystals. What would Kirk say if he walked into the room and saw her like this? she pondered dreamily. Then she shook herself mentally and rubbed herself all over with the bath sheet, using the brisk movements to dispel her foolishly romantic mood.

By the time she was dressed for dinner in a simple shirtwaister of cream silk, it was almost eight o'clock, so there was no time left for speculating about why Kirk wanted her here, or what Leila would say when she found out. For now, it was enough that fate had given her another chance to be near him. It was up to her to make the most of every moment they had together to try to reawaken his memory.

Kirk was waiting for her at the foot of the stairs when she emerged from her room. 'I thought you might get lost trying to locate the dining room,' he explained. His gaze travelled appreciatively over the flattering lines of the dress with its top buttons left casually undone to reveal just a glimpse of the cleft between her breasts. 'You look lovely tonight.'

A dress very like this had been one of Kirk's favourites before it was destroyed in the fire which burnt out her flat. She had been thrilled to find one so like the first and she wondered if it stirred any memories for him now. 'I'm glad you like it,' she murmured. 'Your housekeeper told me not to dress up.'

He opened a door into a small dining room, and she was relieved to find that the table was set for two. So Leila wouldn't be joining them tonight. He seemed to read Erin's thoughts. 'Leila is asleep, so I thought we'd feel more cosy in this room than in the formal dining room.'

To her surprise, Erin discovered that her hands were shaking as she settled herself into the chair Kirk drew out for her. What on earth was she so nervous about? She felt more like a virgin on her first date than a married woman having dinner with her husband. Perhaps it was because they were virtually strangers to each other now. Then it occurred to her that this may be another way to reach him. If she pretended that they *were* strangers, she might be able to win his love all over again. Given his strong sense of loyalty and honour, it was a gamble, but if it worked . . .

She began to put her plan into action as soon as Mrs Niland served the first course of tomato madrilène. In between sips of the delicious herb-flavoured consommé, she chatted to Kirk as if he was, indeed, a stranger, drawing him out artfully about his work and his plans for the future.

Gradually he began to relax and respond to her gentle probing, shedding the tension which had existed between them since that first moment when he questioned her on the assembly line.

'You're different tonight,' he commented as he leaned across to refill her glass with more of the excellent *brut* champagne.

Erin smiled coyly. 'In what way?'

His gaze softened as he regarded her across the flickering flame of the candle which decorated the centre of the table. She leaned towards him with both forearms resting lightly on the table, aware that the pose thrust her well-formed breasts forward so they pushed against the buttons of her dress.

'I don't know—more relaxed?' he suggested.

She pretended dismay. 'You don't like me to relax?'

He chuckled throatily. 'I didn't say that. Maybe it's because I've only seen you in a business setting lately that I even noticed it.'

She didn't remind him that he had seen her in a very unbusinesslike setting at her apartment, the night he made love to her. She didn't want to destroy the fragile harmony which existed between them at present. 'You're probably right,' she agreed. 'Maybe getting away from the office was a good idea.'

'We haven't exactly got away from the office,' he reminded her. 'Since we've brought it all with us.'

'But this is a much more pleasant setting to work in, surely?'

He seemed surprised by her change in attitude. 'I suppose it is an attractive place, although I've never really felt at home here.'

Hope flared in her breast. So he, too, felt the coldness of the mansion despite its grandeur. At least some part of him was aware that he didn't really belong here. 'What makes you say that?' she asked idly, although her heart beat faster as she waited for his response.

He twirled the wine-glass absently between long fingers, and stared at the flickering candle flame through the sparkling fluid. 'I don't really know, it's just a feeling I have.'

'How much do you know about your background?' she queried, still keeping her tone deliberately casual.

Instead of the angry reaction she half expected, Kirk surprised her by taking a thoughtful swallow of his wine and staring into the candle flame as if mesmerised. 'Not a hell of a lot,' he began. She held her breath and gripped the stem of her crystal goblet so tightly she was afraid she might snap it. 'It's all a black void until the moment when I came to on the beach, to find Leila bending over me.'

'And you don't remember anything after that?' she ventured.

'Vague ghost shapes, snatches of music—it's like trying to get a grip on quicksilver.'

'Surely Leila can tell you about yourself,' she said with studied sweetness.

He smiled thinly. 'That's the irony of it. She would, but she doesn't know very much herself. It seems I was an itinerant, working my way around Australia, when we met. Love at first sight, she tells me. Unfortunately, I hadn't got around to telling her the name of my home town before I had the accident, otherwise I could have gone back to try and put the pieces together from there.'

Erin had to admire the other woman's cleverness. For whatever reason, she had completely convinced Kirk that they were married and had even fabricated a past for him which would deter him from doing too much digging.

What baffled Erin was *why* Leila would want to do such a thing. With her beauty and advantages, she should have had any number of suitors. The more she thought about it, the more bewildering the whole thing became. 'It must have been a lavish wedding,' she said. 'But I don't suppose you remember any of that either?'

He toyed with his wine glass again before refilling hers and his own. 'Actually, we eloped. Leila told me she didn't want any fuss, and because of her place in society, it would have been unavoidable.'

'Then there wouldn't be any wedding pictures, I suppose,' said Erin with a calculated edge of disappointment in her voice.

'As a matter of fact, there are,' he surprised her by saying. 'I'd be happy to show them to you, but Leila keeps them in her room and I'd hate to disturb her when she's finally getting some rest.'

At this, a chill invaded Erin's body. How could Leila possibly have pictures of a wedding which could not have taken place? Shock made her sway in her chair and Kirk came out of his seat at once to steady her. 'You should go easy on that champagne,' he said in concern.

'I'm all right, really,' she tried to reassure him, but without much conviction.

He grasped her chin in one hand and turned her face up to his. 'You don't sound all right. If it isn't the champagne, are you sure you aren't ill?'

Not unless you count sick at heart, she thought. 'I'm fine,' she said aloud. His touch, aided perhaps by the champagne they had both drunk, fired her senses with passion, but it was a luxury she dared not give in to, not here under Leila Coventry's own roof. 'Please, let me go,' she pleaded.

But he kept his steadying arm around her shoulders. His hand moved from her chin to caress the line of her jaw. Then, very slowly, he urged her to her feet. Her chair tumbled backwards, but neither of them noticed it fall. They were too intent on the tension that stretched between them like a tangible thing.

For a moment they stood like statues, mesmerised by the strength of the emotions being telegraphed between them. With an oath, Kirk closed the small remaining distance between them and crushed her to him.

'No, don't,' she protested unconvincingly. Here in his arms was the only place in the world she wanted to be. But not like this, not because he thought she was a temptress he was too weak to resist. She tried to squirm free, but she was pressed tightly against him, alarmingly conscious that he was so aroused he was beyond caring that Leila was in the house. She tried to reason with him. 'What if someone comes?'

'Who?' he muttered with his mouth buried in the silken strands of her hair. 'Ethel will be watching television in her room by now, and Leila is fast asleep.'

But the housekeeper wasn't watching television, Erin discovered to her mortification. As Kirk bent to kiss her again, she caught a glimpse of black moving quickly out of sight past the doorway. 'Oh no!' she gasped.

He looked at her worriedly. 'What's the matter?'

She stared fixedly at the door. 'I think Mrs Niland was watching us.'

With one hand, he ruffled her hair. 'You're imagining things.'

'No, I'm sure I saw her just now.'

His frown deepened and his eyes flashed scornfully at her. 'Now I know you, Erin Wilding!'

Excitement clamoured in her breast and she swung her head up at once. 'You . . . you do?'

'Yes, I know your type. You're nothing but a tease who leads men on until they lose all semblance of control, then you want to back off on some flimsy pretext.'

With a crash, she came back down to earth. For a moment she had been encouraged to think that he remembered her, but he was only confirming his earlier impression of her as an unscrupulous opportunist who used her feminine wiles to get what she wanted. The discovery left an acrid taste in her mouth.

At her crestfallen expression, his mouth tightened into an implacable line. 'A bit too close to home, was I?'

What was the use? She turned away in despair. 'Think what you like, you won't believe me anyway.' At that moment, she realised, she was closer to giving up than she had ever been before. It was heartbreaking to be here, in Kirk's arms, and be unable to make him believe who she was. She might as well be a thousand miles away.

She should have known he didn't really intend to make love to her here while the woman he thought of as his wife was asleep upstairs. He had only been testing Erin, she understood that now. 'I suppose you're happy now,' she said listlessly.

His eyebrows slanted upwards. 'Should I be?'

'Of course. You've convinced yourself that there's

nothing more between us than sexual attraction and that you're strong enough to resist it. Wasn't that what you set out to do?'

He rested his back against the dining room wall, folded his arms across his chest and regarded her steadily. 'No, it wasn't. I hoped that kissing you would awaken some of the feelings I'm supposed to have had for you.'

'But it didn't work.'

'No, it didn't,' he confirmed, and she detected a note of real regret in his voice. 'There is one thing, though . . .'

'Yes?' she prompted without hope.

Before he could go on they were startled by a loud crash from over their heads. 'That came from Leila's room!' exclaimed Kirk in alarm.

He raced out of the room and took the stairs two at a time. Erin followed him more slowly as he went into the bedroom next to hers on the upper floor. It was Leila's room and Erin gained an impression of white Queen Anne style furniture and frilled net curtaining, before her attention was caught by Leila, who lay sobbing on the floor beside her overturned wheelchair.

'What happened?' Kirk asked as he picked her up and placed her carefully in the four-poster bed. The heiress turned her face from him and shed fresh tears into her pillow.

'She tried to stand, that's what happened,' came a cold voice from across the bed. Only then Erin noticed Mrs Niland standing there.

'Couldn't you help her, or stop her?' Kirk demanded.

'I didn't know what she meant to do.'

'I wanted to come downstairs, to you,' Leila said, her voice muffled by the pillow.

Mechanically, Kirk stroked the heiress's damp hair back from her forehead. 'It's all right, I'm here now.'

Erin felt physically ill. She was almost certain that Mrs Niland had reported to Leila at least part of what she had seen in the dining room and that this had precipitated Leila's attempt to get out of bed.

Kirk must have suspected the same thing, because he turned to the housekeeper. 'Did you say anything to upset my wife?'

'As if I would do such a thing!' she defended herself righteously. 'I just told her that Mrs Wilding was here, that's all.'

That was enough, thought Erin. The housekeeper would probably have told Leila a lot more, but she had also been taken by surprise when Leila tried to get up.

'I think you'd both better go and let Leila get some rest,' Kirk said quietly, but in a manner which said he would tolerate no arguments. The housekeeper gave Erin a malevolent look, but left without protest. With a last helpless glance at Kirk who was still stroking Leila's hair, Erin turned on her heel. Some instinct made her pause in the act of opening her own bedroom door and she heard Leila say, 'I don't want her here, darling, please send her away!'

Too sick at heart to wait for Kirk's reply, Erin fled into her own room and stood with her back against the door. She had no doubt who Leila was referring to.

Erin's suitcase still lay in a corner of the room and for a fleeting moment she was tempted to throw her things into it and get away from Eaglewood as fast as she could. But that was exactly what Leila was hoping she would do, to leave the field clear for her with Kirk. If he really loved Leila Coventry, Erin might have been tempted to give in and leave so he could find happiness with the heiress. But he didn't love her, Erin was convinced. He had confessed that he was falling in love with Erin, so the attraction between them was as strong as ever, even though he still couldn't remember their marriage.

This thought gave her some comfort, and slowly she began to undress for bed, knowing that she would go on fighting as long as there was a chance that Kirk might remember her.

CHAPTER SEVEN

ERIN's feet slithered over the dewy crystal grass as she made her way towards the private beach below Eaglewood. It was the first time she had ventured down to the little cove, but this morning she had to have some time to herself before she faced another day in the temporary office she and Kirk had established at the house.

The beach provided just the right atmosphere of peace and tranquillity she had been hoping for. The morning haze still lay out over the ocean where it had built up overnight against the headlands, as the waves sent up spray into the light, warm night air.

Ahead of her, the azure water rose and fell tantalisingly, and the crisp, uncrowded early waves broke against the sand with the same simple clarity as the sun's low light.

Looking around the empty sands, disturbed by only a few footprints from some early morning jogger, she sighed with satisfaction. This was the balm her troubled soul needed.

For the last week since Erin had overheard Leila begging Kirk to send her away from Eaglewood, she had felt acutely uncomfortable in the other woman's household. Twice, she had suggested to Kirk that it might be better if he brought one of the other secretaries out here to work with him, but—perversely, Erin thought—he had refused, giving his original excuse that the Americans preferred to deal with her.

There had been no repetition of the moment when Kirk had kissed her with unreserved passion during her first dinner here. Erin wondered if he knew that the housekeeper was watching their every move, and almost certainly reporting back to Leila. Was that the reason why he kept his distance, emotionally as well as physically? Or was he now satisfied that, because kissing Erin had failed to stir his memory, they had no shared past to remember?

This thought was so painful that she banished it by shedding her terry-towelling wrap in one lithe movement and diving straight into the beckoning waves.

A few moments later she surfaced, breathless but cleansed by the rippling waves which massaged her skin to tingling life. The water still had a night-cool edge, although the sun was rapidly warming the shallows, but she welcomed the coldness for its cathartic effect.

How had she got herself into this mess? It hardly seemed possible that only a month had passed since she first glimpsed Kirk's picture in the society pages. It had seemed so simple then. She had never dreamed that his amnesia would drive such a wedge between them, or that it would have sent him into the arms of another woman.

She shivered with more than the water's chill as she thought about Kirk in Leila's arms. Erin had never believed herself capable of violence and had been unsympathetic of people convicted of so-called 'crimes of passion'. But in the last month she had come to understand the intensity of the feelings which drove people to commit such crimes. Never before had she experienced such insane jealousy as when she was forced to watch Leila with Kirk. Erin was not proud of her own feeings at such times, but she was incapable of holding them back.

Righteous anger welled within her now, just thinking about it. In a fury, she hurled her body into the waves and struck out farther and farther from the shore, her arms and legs pumping like pistons as she churned through the water. Only when her legs began to feel leaden and unresponsive did she pause to tread water, and her chest heaved from the exertion.

Suddenly a cold stab of fear went through her. Only feet away, a long black shape torpedoed through the water towards her. Shark! Ever since she was a child, she had been terrified of these killers of the deep, but had overcome her dread sufficiently so she could enjoy the pleasures of the surf. Now the sight of the black shape awakened her childhood fears again.

Frantically she struck out for the shore, which now seemed a million miles away. But she was already tired from the long swim out and each stroke demanded more and more effort. Meanwhile, the black shape came inexorably closer and she panicked when her arms refused to obey her. She knew it was the end when the water closed over her head and the black shape caught up with her.

'Hey, don't faint on me! It's a long swim back!'

Unbelievably, her head was lifted clear of the water again and she opened her eyes to find herself cradled in Kirk's arms as he trod water. He was clad in a sleek black wetsuit with a snorkelling outfit dangling from his neck.

'I thought you were a . . . a . . . shark,' she gasped as soon as she could speak again. Then reaction made her furiously angry. 'Why on earth didn't you call out to me, or . . . or surface?' she demanded. 'I could have had a heart attack and drowned!'

'Because I didn't think you were silly enough to mistake a diver in a wetsuit for a shark,' he retorted.

If he hadn't been holding her so tightly she would have started to swim away from him at once. 'Me—be silly enough?' she splutterd. 'Of all the bigheaded, unthinking . . .'

He clamped a wet hand over her mouth and she had to fight for breath as salt water trickled between her lips. 'Enough!' he commanded. 'I'm sorry I frightened you—all right?'

Her eyes were as round as saucers above the hand he still held clamped over her mouth, but she nodded, feeling tears of frustration prickle behind her eyes.

Gently he removed his hand. 'I really am sorry, believe me. I didn't mean to frighten you.'

'It's all right—as you say, I shouldn't have been so silly,' she said flatly.

He studied her sceptically, as if sensing that she wasn't finished yet. 'Perhaps we'd better swim back to the beach,' he suggested.

Since he still held her against his chest she was only too happy to comply. Even with the slippery black wetsuit between them she was alarmingly conscious of his hard, muscular contours and the way his heart pounded rhythmically against her breasts as he supported her in the water.

Fortunately, he released her and they swam stroke for stroke back to the beach. She was sure he could have covered the distance in half the time alone, but he matched his pace to hers and they reached the shallows together.

Tiredness and the aftermath of shock made her stumble when she tried to stand, but she shrugged off the arm he tried to put around her. 'I can manage, thanks,' she snapped at him, and forced herself to make reasonably steady progress to the part of the beach where she had left her towel.

Kirk pulled a towel out from a rock crevice where he must have left it earlier, and unrolled it alongside hers. She tried not to look as he unzipped the wetsuit and stepped out of it, but her eye was drawn to his athletic shape outlined in the briefest of navy blue swimming trunks. The snorkelling outfit was dropped carelessly on to the sand, then he stretched out beside her on the towel.

'Out with it!'

'Out with what?' she asked coolly.

'You're bottling something up, I can tell. And it's not just your anger because I gave you a fright. I've already apologised about that.'

'And I accepted,' she agreed levelly.

'So what's eating you?'

'If you must know, it's being watched every minute by that eagle-eyed housekeeper of Leila's.'

He stared at her in astonishment. 'You can't mean dear old Ethel?'

'Dear old Ethel,' she mimicked, not caring whether she sounded bitchy or not. 'Dear old Ethel, as you call her, can't get me out of Leila's house quickly enough!'

His expression became stony. 'This time you're going too far, Erin. I was prepared to be tolerant when your fantasies were limited to our supposed love affair, but when you start involving an innocent old lady, I have to insist that you stop it.'

'How long have you known Mrs Niland?' Erin persisted.

'Since before Leila and I were married, as it happens,' he said in the same unyielding tone.

She stared at him, shaken. '*Before* you were married?'

'Yes. I'm sorry if that puts paid to your theory that my relationship with Leila only started with my amnesia. You see, her father didn't approve of her seeing someone outside her own social orbit, so Ethel Niland acted as our go-between.'

'You remember that?' Erin asked tensely.

'Obviously not, but you can't call them *both* liars, surely.'

Can't I? thought Erin grimly. If the so-called witness to Kirk's romance with Leila had been anyone else, Erin might have begun to doubt her own sanity, but she was convinced that Mrs Niland would go to any lengths to protect her beloved Coventry family, so she could only suppose the housekeeper and Leila were somehow in league to deceive Kirk as to who he really was. Couldn't Kirk see how devoted Mrs Niland was to Leila?

He watched her interplay of emotions which she was unable to keep from showing on her face. 'Despite what I've said, you're going to stick to your story, aren't you?'

'I'm going to stick to the truth,' she repeated like a litany. In anguish, she jumped to her feet and snatched up her wrap and towel. 'What's the use? I'm going to get ready for work.'

Kirk rose more slowly, uncoiling from the sand like a snake preparing to strike. 'As you like, although I wish you'd stop this charade and be reasonable.'

'Be reasonable?' she cried. 'You're the one who isn't being reasonable. The least you could do is investigate my "story", as you call it.'

'I've already investigated it in the best way I know how, and it hasn't done any good.'

She flushed scarlet. He was referring to the passionate way he had kissed her at dinner when she first came to Eaglewood. It had aroused a flood of tender memories in her, and it had stirred something in him, she could swear to it. If they hadn't been interrupted by Leila, she was sure he would have started to remember. She turned and began to trudge back up the beach feeling as if the sun had gone in, although the day had been bright with promise earlier.

He caught her arm. 'Erin . . .'

'Yes, what is it?'

'I'd like us to be friends.'

She pulled her arm free and shook her head in disbelief. How could he possibly think they could be mere friends? 'No,' she rasped, 'I can't settle for that.' Not when they had been lovers, she thought despairingly as she stumbled away from him.

Behind her there came a loud splash and she guessed that he had dived back into the water to try to work off some of his annoyance with her in the surf. It was all so hopeless. He should understand that if she had been a confidence trickster, she could never have stuck to her story so tenaciously for so long. Somewhere along the line she would have been bound to contradict herself or say something which would have branded her a fake. She knew she hadn't done that—how could she, when she had only told him the truth?

Her store of medical knowledge was limited, gleaned from various spells as a temporary secretary to doctors, but she did know that amnesia was sometimes the mind's defence against an unpleasant truth. Was that how Kirk subconsciously thought of their marriage—as a fact too unpleasant to face? Could that be why he so stubbornly refused to give her the benefit of the doubt?

She hadn't noticed that she was crying until something splashed wetly onto the front of her bikini. Angrily she dashed the tears away. She and Kirk *had* been happy, she was certain of it. No, there had to be something else which his mind refused to accept and which stopped him from acknowledging her as his wife. But what? Her head ached as she tried to think of an answer, but by the time she had reached the house, she was no closer to a solution.

'Ethel? Ethel, where are you?'

The petulant voice drew Erin's attention as she climbed the stairs, intending to go and change before making her way to the temporary office. Leila's room adjoined hers and it was from here that the voice was coming. Erin hesitated. She didn't want to see any more of Leila than she had to, but if the woman needed help it would be uncharitable to ignore her calls—she was crippled, after all.

Reluctantly, Erin moved towards Leila's room. 'Is there something you need?' Her voice tailed off as she came face to face with the heiress. 'You can walk!'

At the sound of Erin's voice, Leila whirled away from the dressing table and faced her accuser defiantly. Her legs were rock-steady under her and if it hadn't been for the wheelchair which now stood neglected in a corner, Erin would have had trouble believing that Leila had been paralysed until yesterday. A cold sensation crept over her. *If* she had been paralysed. 'This was all a trick, wasn't it?' she asked in a low, strangled tone. 'You were able to walk all along, weren't you?'

Leila's eyes glittered strangely, making Erin wonder if the other woman had been drinking, despite the early hour. 'No, it wasn't a trick, not at first,' Leila said with a brittle laugh. 'I got some feeling back two days ago. It hurt like the very devil, if it gives you any satisfaction. Then gradually, I found that my legs would support me and ... *voilà*!' She performed a mocking curtsey at Erin, then clutched the edge of the dressing table. 'Whoops! The technique needs a bit more work, I'm afraid.'

She *had* been drinking, or else she was still influenced by the medication which had been prescribed for her after the accident, Erin thought. She looked at Leila in bewilderment. 'Why did you let everyone think you were still paralysed?'

Leila laughed again, this time with a grating sound that reminded Erin of a fingernail being pulled across a blackboard. 'You have to ask *me* that? I should have thought you, of all people, would understand why I had to do it!'

Erin felt the colour drain from her face and she

clenched her hands so tightly together that her fingernails bit painfully into her palms. 'You do know who I am,' she said almost inaudibly.

Slowly and stiffly, Leila made her way across the room and sank down on to the edge of the big Queen Anne bed. 'Of course I do. I read your personnel file at Sands Engineering. It wasn't very clever of you to be so honest about everything. You should learn to be more devious, darling.'

Coming from such an incongruous source, the endearment made Erin wince. 'You know all about being devious, of course,' she couldn't help retorting.

In an instant the deceptive softness fled from Leila's expression. 'Too right, I do. When you've had to fight for everything you've got, you soon learn that being nice seldom pays.'

'Fight for everything? But surely . . .' Lost for words, Erin spread her hands wide to encompass the lavishly furnished room. How could anyone who possessed so much have to fight for anything?

Leila followed the direction of Erin's gesture. 'You wouldn't understand. Like everyone else, you think I had the Coventry Corporation handed to me on a plate. Well, I didn't.'

In confusion, Erin sought the support of an upholstered boudoir chair, fearing that her legs might give out on her if she didn't sit down. 'I don't understand. What has that got to do with me . . . and Kirk?'

Leila's head came up and her defiant gaze raked Erin's face, making her flinch as if from a blow. 'It has everything to do with . . . Don,' she said, her flashing eyes daring Erin to correct her. Erin willed herself to wait in silence. With a taut smile of satisfaction, Leila rewarded her with more information. 'You may think you know who that man is, but I can assure you he is as much my creation as any product of Sands Engineering, or any other division of the Corporation.'

The blood began to pound in Erin's temples, causing a singing sensation in her ears which made her feel dizzy and ill. 'How can you say such a thing?' she cried wildly. 'You can't meddle with a man's life just because it suits your purpose!'

'Can't I? One of the things I learned while I was still in my cradle is that a Coventry can do anything,' Leila responded. She folded her arms across her chest. 'Shall I tell you how I created Don Sands?'

Erin didn't want to listen, but she knew she had no choice if she was to make sense of this nightmare. Only when she knew the whole story could she decide what to do next. 'I'm listening,' she said, amazed that she could sound so calm.

'It was like this,' Leila began in the manner of an indulgent parent telling a story to a child, 'until he died three years ago, my father was the most successful businessman this country has known.'

Erin nodded. Like most people, she knew the well-publicised legend which had grown up around Henry Coventry's career. He had started work as a lad of fourteen, running errands in a small factory that made bicycle parts. Before he was twenty he had saved enough to buy the business on a small down payment with the balance to be paid out of the profits, and had begun the daring programme of expansion which made the Coventry Corporation into one of the largest and most diversified manufacturing groups in Australia. It was Henry Coventry's personal monument.

Leila watched Erin's face closely. 'I see you do know the story. But what nobody outside the Head Office knew was that, for the last five years of H.C.'s life, I was his right-hand man.' She didn't seem to notice that she used a male pronoun to describe herself. 'I practically ran the Corporation at the end.'

Although Leila's digression into a history of the company was making Erin burn with impatience, she was momentarily distracted by this last statement. The news of Henry Coventry's failing health had only been made public after his death. Though there was speculation as to how he had managed to control his business so successfully despite what was later revealed as a critical illness, there had been no mention in the newspapers of his daughter stepping in and taking over.

'Surprises you, doesn't it?' the heiress said smugly. 'It surprised a lot of people when they found out I could not only run the show as well as H.C., but in many ways I could do it better.'

The venom in Leila's voice made Erin reel back instinctively. 'I still don't see what this has got to do with Kirk.'

'As I said—everything. My father loved having me work alongside him. But in the end, he left everything to my brother Tom.' She was unable to keep the bitterness out of her voice. 'My little brother, the sheep farmer—who wouldn't know a convertible note from a cowbail!'

In spite of herself, Erin felt a surge of sympathy for the other woman, whose distress was all too evident. It was the first time Erin had seen a glimpse of the real Leila Coventry under the glossy veneer, and it was obvious that the tough exterior hid a mass of emotional wounds. 'Why would your father do such a thing if he knew you loved the business and were good at running it?'

Leila's eyes glittered with unexpected tears. 'He did it for my own good,' she said flatly. 'Oh, it was all spelled out in his will. He knew how like him I was and he said he didn't want me to make the same mistake he had—sacrificing my whole life to the Corporation. He couldn't know I had already done that—and he made it a condition that I could only inherit if I was married.'

Slowly, realisation began to dawn on Erin. 'So when you found Kirk on the beach and discovered he had amnesia, you decided to pass him off as your husband so you could inherit the business. I see.'

Leila pressed her hands tightly together in an unconscious gesture of supplication. 'No, you don't see. I only wanted what was rightfully mine.'

'What about the life which was rightfully Kirk's?' Erin demanded. How could Leila possibly believe that what she had done was justified?

'He didn't *have* a life, or at least, none that he could remember. He was a very sick, confused man when I found him. If I hadn't given him some shred of a past to cling to, he would have gone crazy.'

'But you gave him much more than a shred. You gave him a completely fraudulent background!' Erin cried. 'You must have known that the authorities were searching for him and that I . . . that I . . .' she broke off, unable even now, to describe the agony she had endured during the dark days of the search, when Kirk's fate was still unknown.

'The papers never mentioned a wife,' Leila said as if that ended the argument.

'Then you didn't read many papers,' Erin snapped angrily. She could never make Leila understand the havoc her actions had caused in Erin's life, to say nothing of Kirk's. What would he say when he found out he had been deceived into living a lie to satisfy Leila's ambitions? 'Weren't you afraid someone would recognise him?' she asked Leila.

'Luckily, as it turned out, he didn't know too many people in this city. The few who tried to get close to him soon found it was more profitable to agree that they were mistaken. Then I let him meet just enough of the cranks to be convinced that he had no hope of finding anyone who genuinely remembered him. You didn't have any luck, did you?'

Erin looked away, aware of just how thorough Leila had been. 'His memory might have come back. Weren't you worried about that?' she tried again.

Leila tossed her blonde hair in a girlish gesture which was at odds with her calculating actions. 'No, that was one thing I didn't have to worry about.'

'But how could you be so confident? Any little thing could trigger his memory even now.'

Leila stood up and limped to the window, where she gripped the sill to steady herself and looked out across the vast grounds of Eaglewood like a monarch surveying her kingdom. After a long pause, she turned to Erin again. 'Nothing is going to trigger his memory, so you may as well stop hoping!'

Erin looked wildly around. 'How can you say that? You're not a doctor.' She jumped up. 'I insist that you call Kirk and tell him what you've told me. Maybe if he hears the truth from you . . .'

'All right, I'll tell him if you insist,' Leila capitulated, but so readily that Erin's suspicions were aroused.

'You—you will?' she quavered.

'Sure, if you want to get back a gibbering wreck of a man.'

Erin's legs felt as if they were rooted to the floor. She stared at Leila in bewilderment, then ran a hand through her hair distractedly. 'What are you talking about?'

'I think you already know, but I'll spell it out for you anyway. The doctors tell us that if Don is pressured too hard into trying to remember his past, it could completely destroy his mind.' At the look of horror she observed on Erin's face, she nodded. 'I see you know what I'm getting at.'

Numbly, Erin was forced to nod agreement as she remembered the agony Kirk had endured when she played 'their' record at her flat. But even if the strain of trying to remember caused him pain, surely it wasn't powerful enough to destroy his mind? 'No, it can't be true! You're lying,' she ground out.

'There's only one way to find out,' Leila flung at her. 'I don't think you will want to take that risk.'

Leila was right. The only way Erin could test the truth of her statement was to force Kirk to go on trying to remember, and if Leila wasn't bluffing ... the price was just too high. The idea of Kirk being reduced to a vegetable, his fine mind robbed of its reasoning power, was unthinkable. He wouldn't want to go on living like that. Erin knew she was finally beaten. She buried her face in her hands and sobbed silently, her shoulders heaving.

Leila watched her pitilessly. 'I knew you would make the right choice.'

Through her tears, Erin looked up at the heiress. 'What other choice do I have?'

Leila shrugged. 'I would have taken the gamble, but that's the difference between us, honey.'

Every nerve in Erin's body protested at the thought of giving Kirk up to this creature whose heart seemed to have been cast in one of her own foundries. But it was precisely because she loved Kirk that she knew she had no other choice. With her own eyes she had seen the pain he endured when he tried to remember their shared past. Why this should be, she had no idea—and no prospect, now, of ever finding out. She only knew she could not be the instrument of his destruction. His powerful intellect and razor-sharp wit were part of what made him the man she loved. Without that, he would be an empty shell, a shadow of a man to be nursed, fed ... no! her mind screamed a protest. At least with Leila, he had a chance at happiness, and Erin had to grant him that.

'I'll leave this afternoon,' she said dully, and turned to go.

Before she could escape to her room, a figure darkened the doorway and she cannoned into Kirk. He had changed into grey chambray jeans and a Western shirt, and his hair was still slick from his swim. Erin's heart constricted at the sight of him and she fought an urge to throw herself at him and cling to him like a child. She had to remember that her own peace of mind was the price she had just agreed to pay for his continued wellbeing. She shrank back against the doorframe to allow him to go past her into the room.

When she cringed away from him, he frowned, then his attention was captured by the sight of Leila standing unaided by the window.

At once, Leila hurled herself at him. 'I can walk, darling—isn't it wonderful?'

He held her at arm's length, a smile lighting his even features. 'It certainly is! When did this happen?'

'I just found out,' said Leila, giving Erin a challenging look. 'I've felt some movement for a couple of days now, but I was afraid to say anything in case nothing came of it.'

Leila's imitation of a clinging vine was in such contrast to her icy self-assurance a moment ago that Erin felt slightly ill. How could she fight someone who had no scruples at all, especially when the price was Kirk's sanity?

Her despair must have shown on her face, because Kirk looked at her in surprise. 'What's wrong, Erin? Aren't you happy that Leila can walk again?'

'Of course,' she said stiffly, feeling trapped.

'Then what's the matter?'

Before Erin could reply, Leila cut in, drawing closer to Kirk as if to symbolically align herself with him against Erin. 'I'll tell you what's the matter,' she said venomously. 'Erin came in here to try to blackmail me!'

Erin stared at Leila in shocked surprise, and felt her blood turn to ice. This was a twist she hadn't anticipated. 'Blackmail?' she repeated stupidly.

Kirk's pleased smile was replaced by a look of cold fury. 'What are you talking about, Leila?'

She gripped his arm urgently. 'Erin threatened to tell the Americans that she's really your wife. You know how touchy John Burrows is—the first hint of a scandal like that and the whole deal would be off!'

He ignored the last part of Leila's tirade to turn to Erin. 'Is any of this true?'

Erin's heart sank. So Leila meant to keep her under control using the one weapon that was a hundred per cent effective—Kirk's sanity. As long as Leila possessed the power to drive Kirk over the edge, she could make Erin do her bidding. It seemed she meant to use that power to the full. Even so, Erin couldn't let her get away with such a blatantly untrue accusation. 'I . . . I did tell Leila I was your wife, but . . .'

'You see?' Leila interrupted triumphantly. 'She doesn't even try to deny it!'

'What could she possibly stand to gain from such a claim?' Kirk asked coldly.

'A quarter of a million dollars.'

Erin's gasp was involuntary. Surely Kirk couldn't think she would do such a thing? And yet Leila had played her cards very cleverly. Kirk had been wondering why Erin persisted in her claim to be his wife against all odds, now he had an all-too-plausible explanation. He studied her coldly as a scientist might examine a particularly unappealing creature under a microscope, and she could almost hear him working it out. He would think that Erin had deliberately made herself popular with the Americans so her blackmail threat would be doubly effective. In her turn, Leila would be counting on Erin's love of Kirk to prevent her defending herself.

In this, Leila was right. Erin longed to be able to cry out that it was all a cruel lie, that she would do anything in the world rather than hurt the man she loved. But if she did, he would want to know the rest and she couldn't risk hurting him, no matter what it cost her.

'Don't you have anything to say?' he demanded.

She looked down at the carpet. 'No, I . . . I have nothing to say.'

'I see.'

'No, you don't see,' she wanted to cry out, but remembering what was at stake, she forced herself to remain silent while Leila watched her with an expression of triumph on her face.

'I told you no good would come of bringing her here,' Leila said smugly. 'I was right, wasn't I?'

'So it seems,' he said shortly, and turned dark eyes on Erin. His expression was unfathomable, but she couldn't say whether he was angry with her or sad that she had betrayed his trust in her. Either way, it meant the same thing. He wouldn't want to go on working with her after this, even if Leila would permit it. So even that slim bond between them would be severed, ending for ever any chance for him to remember Erin and acknowledge her as his wife.

Her heart ached to think of him at the mercy of someone as cold and unfeeling as Leila. No one knew better than Erin the depth and warmth of Kirk's emotions; the passions he had aroused in her so often before he disappeared. She knew there would never be another man for her as long as Kirk still lived.

He lived, she reminded herself. At least she had that knowledge to comfort her in the empty days ahead. At least he was safe and well. It wasn't much, but it was infinitely better than the black void she had endured before, not knowing whether he was dead or alive. She must cling to that. Wanly she smiled, then realised how he must interpret her smile.

'You little bitch!' he swore under his breath as he turned abruptly away.

When she looked up again he was gone, too disgusted, she imagined, even to stay in the same room with her. He couldn't have known that her smile was a pathetic attempt to obtain what comfort she could from the knowledge that at least he was safe and well. He had interpreted it as bravado in the face of her accusers, and he had walked out in disgust. His last comment showed clearly what he thought of her now.

Bleakly, she covered her face with her hands, then opened her eyes again when Leila chuckled throatily. 'You should have been an actress,' she said. 'I knew you wouldn't contradict me after our little ... er ... discussion, but I didn't expect you to condemn yourself so thoroughly.'

With a cry of despair, Erin fled from the room.

CHAPTER EIGHT

IF she had to draft one more letter confirming an order, she would scream! Erin decided as her fingers plodded doggedly over the keyboard of her typewriter. She looked around her, but the other girls in the secretarial pool didn't seem to share her sense of desperation. She supposed they considered themselves lucky to have a job which could take them to any part of the company at a moment's notice. Although the work was basically the same, no matter which executive they were assigned to, each change of surroundings provided at least a brief escape from the mind-numbing routine.

For what seemed like the hundredth time that afternoon, she typed the words, 'Yours faithfully, G. M. de Salle, Engineering Division, Coventry Corporation,' and added the letter to the growing pile which awaited her current boss, Gordon de Salle's, signature.

She had not expected to have anything more to do with the Corporation after her confrontation with Leila at Eaglewood, which seemed to have taken place two years ago instead of only two weeks. After that devastating scene during which Leila had revealed how easily Kirk's mental stability could be destroyed if he was pressured into remembering his past, Erin knew that for his sake, she couldn't take the risk of staying near him any longer. With his last, cruel remark ringing in her ears, she had been packing to leave Eaglewood when Leila appeared in her bedroom doorway.

'Not so fast! I want you somewhere where I can keep my eye on you.'

In dismay, Erin straightened from her suitcase and stared at Leila. Hadn't she done enough damage to Erin already without wanting to prolong their relationship? 'What do you want me to do?' she asked.

'I want you to go on working for the Corporation,' Leila told her calmly. 'There's only a month remaining before the merger date when Don and I transfer our activities to the United States. After that, you can do whatever you like.'

The room tilted crazily around Erin and she sat down abruptly. Surely Leila couldn't expect her to go on working alongside Kirk now she knew there was no possible future for them? 'What kind of a monster are you?' she asked in a hoarse whisper.

Leila's eyes widened in mock surprise. 'Really, darling, what a low opinion you must have of me! Of course I don't mean you to go on working in your present job—I'm not as heartless as all that. Remember, Coventry is a very big organisation. I'll find you a job where you don't even have to see Don again.'

That would suit Leila very well, Erin thought despairingly. By finding Erin a job elsewhere in the corporation, Leila could keep her eye on Erin while ensuring that her path didn't cross with Kirk's before he left for America. 'What sort of job do you have in mind?' she asked listlessly.

Leila wrinkled her brow prettily. 'Let me see. You have impeccable business skills, so I think you would do very well in the secretarial pool at Head Office. Girls come and go there all the time and we have a number of temporary secretaries on call during busy periods, so it won't raise an eyebrow if you suddenly pop up there on Monday.'

So that was that. Erin's immediate future was settled as far as Leila was concerned. Not that it made much difference to Erin. Without Kirk, the future held nothing for her anyway, so she might as well work in Coventry's head office as anywhere. She had almost expected Leila to send her back to the assembly line, but of course, the heiress wouldn't want to take the chance that Erin might meet up with Kirk again. The head office was located in its own building in another part of the Wattle Park industrial estate. Working there, Erin would have little chance of any further contact with Sands Engineering—or its managing director.

There was one thing she had to know. 'Do you love him?' she asked Leila. It was the same question she had put to Kirk, and the way he had evaded it told her all she wanted to know. Now she was curious about Leila's side of things.

Leila's reaction was one of surprise. 'You know, I never even asked myself that,' she confessed. 'When Don was washed up on the beach almost at my feet, he was like the answer to a prayer. It was only later, when I discovered what a great team he and I could make, that I started to feel anything at all for him. It's a luxury I never allowed myself before.'

Her face took on a faraway expression as if she was searching deep within herself for the answer to Erin's question—for herself as much as for Erin. 'When you're born into a family like the Coventrys, you soon find that people will love you for what you have, not for what you are. You can never be sure if the affection you're being offered is genuine or not, so you learn to withhold your own responses in self-defence. When I met Don, he didn't know anything about me or my background. For the first time, I didn't have to hold anything back because I could be sure that he cared for me, not the Coventry fortune.'

'Poor little rich girl,' the thought flashed through Erin's mind. At the same time, she realised with a stab of raw emotion, Leila and Kirk must have become lovers soon after they met. What other interpretation could there be for Leila's statement that she 'hadn't held anything back' where Kirk was concerned? Erin wondered if she would ever quite get used to the idea that Kirk now belonged to Leila in mind and, it seemed she must accept it, in body. The thought was unbelievably painful.

The telephone on her desk shrilled, startling her out of her reverie. She let out a shuddering sigh as she picked up the receiver. 'Erin Wilding here.'

'Ah yes, Erin,' it was Mrs Drake, the supervisor of the secretarial pool. 'I have an assignment for you. I believe you're free this afternoon.'

A glance at the office clock told Erin there was only an hour of the working day remaining. 'Today? But . . .'

'I know it's late, dear, but you will be paid overtime. Mr de Salle tells me he hasn't any more work for you until later in the week.'

There wasn't anything else Erin could say. The extra money would come in handy, of course, but the emotional turmoil of the last few weeks had left her utterly drained and on the brink of exhaustion. The thought of working on into the evening was almost intolerable. 'I did have something planned for tonight,' she said tentatively. It was partly true, she had planned to wash and set her hair.

'That's a shame, but Mr Sands especially asked for you,' Mrs Drake said regretfully.

Mr Sands? Kirk must have traced her to the head office and now he wanted to see her. Could that mean he had finally remembered something? At once, her weariness was forgotten. 'I'll do it,' she said decisively. 'I know where Mr Sands' office is.'

'That's another problem,' Mrs Drake intervened. 'When his assistant put in the request for a pool secretary, she said you were to meet him at a private address on the north shore.'

A little curious but not unduly surprised, Erin wrote down the address Mrs Drake dictated to her. It was not unusual for meetings to be held at the homes of company executives, or in hotels where overseas businessmen were involved. But the address she was given was not that of Eaglewood, and a tremor of excitement ran through her. Kirk must want to ensure that their meeting was a private one. Had he finally discovered what Leila had been up to?

She hardly dared to hope that this could be the case as she freshened up her make-up and brushed her hair until it shone. Fortunately, she had chosen to wear a two-piece summer suit today and the silky fabric looked as fresh as when she first walked into the office that morning.

Humming a little tune to herself, she half-ran down the steps to the main entrance where the taxi she had summoned moments before was waiting for her. No matter how much she disliked her present job, she had to admit it had its advantages, such as transport between assignments by taxi, paid for by the company.

Except that this wasn't the usual secretarial assignment, she reminded herself. Kirk had sent for her and she was on her way to his side.

'You seem very pleased with yourself. On the way to meet the boy-friend?' the taxidriver asked her goodnaturedly.

She smiled back at him. 'Something like that.'

Oh, if only it turned out to be true! As the clusters of suburban houses, and then the imposing grey span of the Harbour Bridge, flashed past, she allowed herself to dream of what it would be like if Kirk had, indeed, regained his memory. It wouldn't be easy, but she knew she could find it in her heart to put these last three years behind her. He had never loved Leila, that was what mattered, so whatever else had happened between him and Leila couldn't be allowed to matter either. Their shared future was what counted. She had a moment's worry over Kirk. But surely no harm could come to him if he had remembered of his own accord, without pressure. She would find out soon enough.

The taxi drew up outside a huge apartment complex overlooking Sydney Harbour. Between the twin towers of the complex, she glimpsed a swimming pool and spa. This must be a very expensive place to live.

So anxious was she to keep her appointment with Kirk that she almost forgot to pay the taxi driver, but he smiled cheerfully when she came running back. 'I hope he's worth it, love,' he winked at her, and drove away.

The doorman was expecting her, it seemed, for he showed her to the lift and told her which button to press, then left her alone in the timber-lined cubicle as it carried her upwards to meet Kirk.

But it was not Kirk who greeted her at the door of the apartment. She pressed the intercom button and waited expectantly for a response, but instead of the words of welcome she thought to hear from Kirk, the speaker remained curiously silent and the door swung inwards, obviously operated from somewhere inside the apartment.

'Ah, Mrs Wilding, I'm so glad you were able to come.'

'You!' she gasped, staring in dismay at the personnel manager, Bert Halstead, who stood in the arched entrance leading to the living room. Before she could give herself time to reconsider, she turned on her heel, but he caught her by the arm.

'Not so fast! I sent for a secretary, and as long as you're on the company payroll, you'll do your job. I'm sure Miss Coventry would back me up on that if she was here.'

Erin drew a sharp breath. Leila couldn't be mixed up in this, could she? It would be just like her. As calmly as she could, she said, 'There's been a misunderstanding, Mr Halstead. I was told it was Mr Sands who had sent for me.'

Halstead's lips stretched into an ugly imitation of a smile. 'I thought that might make a difference.'

'You . . . you deliberately let me think that?'

He nodded. 'Now you're getting the idea.'

A sick feeling took hold of her and her palms felt moist with fear. She had always been afraid that Bert Halstead would one day attempt to take his revenge for the way she had humiliated him at work and at the Spring Ball. She had never dreamed that his rancour would be great enough to prompt him to set a trap for her, as it appeared he had done by letting her think Kirk wanted to see her. Halstead knew she would never have agreed to come if he gave his own name. He must have persuaded one of the girls in the office to call Mrs Drake and pretend to be Kirk's assistant. She couldn't blame the girl, whoever she was. Haltead was not above resorting to blackmail to get his own way. Her hunted gaze flickered to the front door.

'You aren't going anywhere until I say so,' he said, guessing her thoughts. 'This apartment has all the latest gimmicks, including computer-operated door locks, worked from a central console.'

So she was trapped. Her shoulders hunched in resignation but instinct warned her not to let him see how afraid she was. 'We'd better get to work,' she said as coolly as she could.

'Work ... of course,' he leered. 'As it happens, I did organise some paperwork in case anyone thinks to check up. The mix-up over who booked you will be dismissed as a simple clerical error, but it would be more difficult to explain why there was no work to show after I'd requested a secretary to handle an overload. If the girl happens to be overcome with passion for me ... well, I couldn't be held responsible for that, now could I?'

Erin shuddered, this time unable to control the reaction, but her fear seemed to excite him all the more. As he escorted her into the huge living room, she made a mental note of the location of a telephone and began looking around unobtrusively to see if she could find the computer console which worked the front door.

Just as she was shedding her jacket, she spotted the console. It was built into an alcove leading through to what she guessed was a kitchen. While Halstead was pouring them drinks from the apartment's well-stocked bar, she managed to sneak a better look at the keyboard. It looked similar to those found on home computers which, in turn, were simplified versions of the ones she had used during her secretarial career. If she could only have a few minutes alone with the keyboard, she was sure she could work out the commands which would open the door.

'Here you are, my dear,' said Bert with exaggerated grace. She took the brandy he handed her and sipped it, wincing as the fiery liquid stung her throat. 'Dutch courage', she had heard it called somewhere. Now she understood why, and made herself drink a little more.

True to his word, Halstead handed her a file of legal forms which he wanted complete. 'No sense wasting your visit,' he told her.

'I'll need a typewriter,' she said, hoping it wouldn't be available.

'In here,' he grunted, opening a door off the main room. It led to a small study lined with books obviously chosen more for their decorative covers and uniform size than for their contents. One corner was taken up by the antique carved desk on which sat a modern electronic typewriter. She had thought to protest that she couldn't work under such conditions, but her hopes were dashed at the sight of the machine, which was as modern as any she used in the office. Disconsolately, she sat down at the desk. Perhaps she could stretch the work out long enough to make Halstead lose interest in her.

Again he seemed to sense the direction of her thoughts. 'Don't take all night,' he growled. 'Remember, I know your typing speed, so I've a very good idea how long that job should take you.'

He left the room and she breathed a little easier when she heard him moving about the other room. But he was right. She was a fast typist, and there was no way she could make such a simple job last for very long without him becoming suspicious. Besides which, since it was only for appearances' sake, he might well decide that having half the job finished was enough to make his request for a secretary seem justified.

She wondered fleetingly whether she could slip into the living room and try to reach the door controls, but he would be listening for the sound of the typewriter. There was nothing for it but to get started on the work and figure out what to do next afterwards. Perhaps by then he would have had a few more drinks and would be easier to outwit.

Several times while she worked, she heard the clink of bottle against glass, so it seemed this might be her best hope. Still, she couldn't help remembering how drunk he had been at the Spring Ball, and it hadn't prevented him from overpowering her then. If Kirk hadn't come to her aid—she shuddered to think of the consequences. This time, there was no Kirk to rescue her. Apart from Mrs Drake, no one knew where she had gone, and by now most of the staff would have finished work for the day. No one would think of looking for her until morning. She stifled a sob and felt her stomach muscles contract in fearful anticipation. Bert Halstead was a big man and for all his bulk, could move very swiftly. Her chances of being able to escape from him seemed bleak indeed.

'Just about finished, I see,' he said, startling her. She hadn't heard him come in.

'I . . . er . . . some of these have mistakes in them. They should really be retyped,' she improvised.

He rested a hand on her shoulder and she fought the urge to pull away at the contact. There was no sense in provoking him needlessly. 'They're good enough for what I want. Remember, they're only to prove that you came here on a legitimate errand— evidence if you should do such a foolish thing as try to cry rape.'

'I . . . I wouldn't do anything like that.'

He looked at her askance. 'Oh no? And I suppose you'll give in to me willingly, too?' She couldn't even pretend such a thing and she turned her head away. 'I guessed as much! You're as bad as that hoity-toity madam, Leila Coventry. She was all over me until Sands appeared out of nowhere.'

So that was the reason for his hostility. Halstead wasn't after revenge for his humiliation at the Ball, although that was probably part of his motive. More than anything, he wanted to prove to Erin that he was as good a man as Kirk. It was a pity Leila hadn't married Halstead, Erin thought bleakly—they would have been very well matched.

'I gather you don't think much of Don Sands,' she suggested, hoping to divert him a little longer.

She had apparently touched a raw nerve. 'Who does he think he is anyway?' Halstead rasped. 'Come to think of it, that's a good one, since he doesn't know who he is. And yet Leila turns up with his ring on her finger and gives him a wedding present of his own company, named after him and all. Where does that leave me, I ask you?'

'Then she ... she had already agreed to marry you?'

'Not in so many words. But she was interested, I know she was. We just hadn't had the chance to get to know one another properly. It would all have worked out in time, if Sands had just gone back wherever it was he came from.'

'Poor Bert,' said Erin, acting on an inspiration. She put all the sympathy she could contrive into her tone. 'You certainly did get a rough deal, by the sound of things.' She had to fight the churning sensation that started up within her at the touch of his hand, but if she could make him believe she was sympathetic, he might be persuaded to let go.

He tilted his head to one side and looked at her suspiciously. 'That's quite a change of tune, coming from you.'

Hating herself, she patted his hand. 'Yes, but I didn't know the whole story then, did I?'

'No, that's true,' he conceded. 'Of course, very few people know how much I've really contributed to the corporation's success. Never received any credit for it, either. First it was all Henry the wonder-boy, and now it's his daughter. You'd think they were the only people who worked there!'

Listening to the bitterness in his voice, Erin wondered if anyone suspected how Bert Halstead really felt about the Coventrys. He had been with the Corporation since he was fourteen, she had learned during her spell on the assembly line. Obviously he felt that his part in building the huge company should have been much better rewarded. She could hardly believe her luck. If she played on this weakness, she might be able to escape from here unscathed after all.

'Would you mind mixing me another drink, Bert?' she asked sweetly. 'Then you can tell me all about it.'

He studied her sceptically. 'Do you really want to hear?'

She nodded firmly. 'Every word.' If she could encourage him to keep drinking and talking he would probably fall asleep before he had chance to carry out his threat against her.

For the next hour and a half she was treated to a one-sided indictment of the Coventry family. At the end of that time, she knew all about the long, selfless hours Bert Halstead had devoted to helping build up the Corporation, of the personal life he had sacrificed, and the lucrative offers to work elsewhere which he had turned down.

Moodily he swirled the drink around in his glass and stared into it. 'So you can see how I felt when you arrived on the scene, Erin. I really liked you, but all you seemed to care about was Don Sands.'

Erin tensed. This was dangerous ground. 'It's all right, Bert,' she soothed. 'I didn't know what you'd been through. If I had it might have made a difference.'

'You know now. *Does* it make a difference?' he demanded aggressively.

'Well, of course it does. I . . .'

'Liar!' he interrupted angrily and she jumped, mindful of how on edge her nerves were after the seemingly endless hours of wondering what he would do next. 'You think I don't know what you're up to?'

'I . . . I don't understand. I've only been trying to help.'

'Help yourself, you mean.' He towered over her and clamped both wrists under his hands so she was powerless to move. Try as she might to twist her face away, he imprisoned her unwilling lips under his in a violent parody of a kiss which made her feel revolted. Then he pulled her to her feet and crushed her against him.

'I can't breathe!' she protested. His hold did not slacken and she knew he was beyond reasoning, so she took the only course remaining to her and slumped, lifeless, in his arms.

'What the——?' The sudden weight of her caught him by surprise. To her relief, he lowered her inert body back into the chair. Before he could become aware of her tactics, she opened her eyes and sprang out of the chair, ducking smoothly under his arm to put the comforting bulk of the couch between them.

His eyes narrowed and for an instant he looked murderous. Then a smile twisted his lips. 'So this is the way you want to play it—well, I can be as rough as you force me to!'

The threat sent shivers down her spine and she made a speedy resolution not to allow him to come close enough to carry it out. The number of whiskies he had downed while she was working in the study had slowed his reflexes, so it was largely a matter of staying out of his reach. How she was going to get close enough to the computer console to open the front door, she still wasn't sure. The whole evening was like a nightmare—except that it was horribly real.

'Please, Bert, let me go,' she pleaded. 'You'll get into terrible trouble acting like this!'

'It's your word against mine, darling,' he reminded her. 'I sent for a pool secretary to do a legitimate job. I can't help it if they got their wires crossed as to who sent for you—or if you turned out to be panting for me, now could I?'

He was mad, she was sure. But she was very much afraid he might be right. Despite his unsavoury reputation, no one could prove that Erin had been an unwilling participant in this scene. Doubtless Leila Coventry would be only too happy to give evidence as to Erin's wanton character if it was called for. What was she going to do?

Suddenly Bert lunged for her, but as she dodged adroitly out of his way, his foot caught in a sheepskin floor rug. With a crash which reverberated through the flat, he sprawled all his length, hitting his head on the corner of the carved coffee table. Horrified, Erin stared down at his unmoving form.

'Mr Halstead? Bert?' she tried, but there was no response. Oh God, he had killed himself! A chill feeling crept over her and she bunched the knuckles of one hand against her mouth to stop herself from screaming. For what seemed an eternity, she stood like a statue, staring down at Halstead's body. Then another terrifying thought occurred to her. What if she was held responsible for his death?

Something seemed to snap inside her and she moved swiftly to the computer control she had spotted earlier. Her hands shook almost uncontrollably, but with a mighty effort of concentration, she finally found the sequence of commands which opened the front door. When it swung open she sobbed aloud with relief. Gathering up her jacket and bag, she fled from the flat, pulling the door shut behind her.

Hardly aware of what she was doing, she flagged down a passing taxi and climbed into it. The driver gave her a curious glance—and only then she realised how she must look. Her skirt was crumpled and her blouse hung askew where Bert had grabbed for her. The top button had come off in the struggle, revealing the cleft between her breasts. When she fumbled for the compact in her purse, the mirror showed that her hair was in complete disarray. As they drove, she tidied herself up as best she could, thankful that the driver asked no questions. She couldn't have endured any probing right now, however well-meaning.

Once she was safely inside her own flat, the enormity of what had happened caught up with her. The spectre of Bert Halstead sprawled on the floor, apparently lifeless, rose up to haunt her until she wanted to scream. Her flesh crawled where he had pawed her and she drew the back of her hand across her bruised mouth to try to erase the feel of his lips on hers.

On a sudden impulse, she threw her bag down on the couch and began to strip off her crumpled clothes, letting them fall on the floor around her feet. Then she went into the bathroom and stood for ages under a shower that was as hot as she could bear, trying to sluice away the sullied feeling she had after Halstead's rough handling of her.

After she had lathered every inch of herself thoroughly and washed her hair with fragrant shampoo, she began to feel calmer. She was still shocked by the evening's events, but she could see

now that she had made a mistake in running away
from Halstead's flat. She should have called the police
at once. By running away, she had made things look
much worse for herself.

Yet she had done nothing wrong, she told herself
angrily. She resolved to get in touch with the police as
soon as she was dressed again. Surely they would
listen to her side of the story.

She had just shrugged into a skimpy bathrobe
and was towelling her hair dry when the doorbell
rang. She froze, a wave of panic washing over her.
Could that be the police already? Perhaps a neighbour of Halstead's had reported the disturbance.
Someone must have seen her drive away in the
taxi.

The doorbell pealed again and she told herself she was
being foolish. It was probably only a neighbour come
to borrow some milk or something. Chiding herself,
she went to the door and opened it.

'Kirk, what are you doing here?' she gasped.

'Never mind that—are you all right?'

'Of course I am, I was just taking a shower.'

'So I see.' Appreciatively, he scanned her slender
figure outlined in the brief robe and the frankness of
his appraisal made her gather the robe defensively
around herself.

'Mind if I come in?'

Without waiting for her answer, he stepped through
the small hallway into the living room, and his all-
encompassing gaze included the clothing scattered
across the floor. With a frown of concern, he took her
shoulders in his hands. 'Are you quite sure you're all
right?'

'You asked that before. Why?'

'Because I've come from Bert Halstead's place.'

'Oh!' She put a hand to her mouth, then at once her
meagre defences crumbled and she sagged against

him. 'I . . . I didn't want to see him dead. I just wanted him to leave me alone.'

'Dead? What are you talking about?'

'When I left him, he was . . . he fell and hit his head. Isn't he . . .?' She was aware she wasn't making much sense, but she seemed incapable of assembling her thoughts in any coherent order.

'He's very much alive,' said Kirk, frowning. 'What made you think he was dead?'

'When he didn't get up, I thought . . . oh, Kirk, I was so frightened!'

'What the devil made you go to his flat in the first place?' he demanded.

Haltingly, Erin explained about the request for a pool secretary which had supposedly come from Don Sands. Kirk's mouth tightened into a grim line at this, but he said nothing, gesturing for her to go on. When she reached the moment when Halstead had tried to attack her, Kirk's hands tightened their grip on the arms of his chair. 'I was wondering whether I should have treated Halstead so harshly. Now I'm sorry I wasn't rougher with him than I was,' he growled.

She looked at him, open-mouthed. 'I don't understand. What do you mean about treating him harshly?'

'Like you, I should probably start at the beginning. I was furiously angry when I discovered that you'd taken off from Eaglewood without a word of explanation. Leila said she didn't know where you'd gone and you didn't answer your phone, so I assumed you'd moved away altogether. It was only when someone reported seeing you at Head Office that I discovered you were still with the Corporation. This afternoon, when I asked the supervisor where I could find you, she seemed very surprised.'

'Of course,' Erin interrupted. 'Mrs Drake thought I'd gone to see you.'

'When she finally gave me the address you'd been sent to, I recognised it as one of Halstead's pied-à-terres. Together with the mystery of who had booked you, it made a very disturbing picture. So I went over there right away. I'm only sorry I didn't get there sooner.' Gently, he fingered the line of her jaw and she winced as he touched a tender spot. Thanks to Halstead's rough treatment, she would probably have a bruise there tomorrow.

'I'm sorry you didn't get there sooner, too,' she said ruefully.

'But it seemed you coped very well on your own, because I found Halstead laid out on the floor.'

'Oh, but I didn't . . .'

'Relax,' he said quickly, 'I'm only teasing, but I can see you aren't in the mood for that after the night you've had. Anyway, when he was coherent again, Halstead told me he'd been drinking and had fallen *after* you left, he assured me. In my effort to get the truth out of him I . . . er . . . did a little damage to myself.' He massaged the knuckles of his right hand significantly.

'You hit him?' Erin said in astonishment.

'Let's say I fired him from the Corporation rather forcefully,' Kirk corrected, smiling for the first time. 'I've had about all I can take from him, and this is the last straw. He has only himself to blame. He's lucky he isn't headed for gaol.'

'And I thought I'd killed him when he fell,' Erin said in wonder. 'I was about to call the police and turn myself in when you arrived.' A new thought occurred to her that sent goosepimples up and down her spine and made the small hairs on the back of her neck stand up. 'What I don't understand is why you were looking for me. After what you said at Eaglewood, I thought you never wanted to see me again.'

'Well, you thought wrong. You and I have to have a long talk.'

CHAPTER NINE

A LUMP rose in Erin's throat and threatened to choke her. 'Have you remembered something?' she asked, and took a deep breath to try to calm the fluttering sensation in her chest.

Kirk sighed heavily. 'I wish to God I had, then all this would be over and done with.'

'What do you mean—"all this"?'

'The mystery of my past. *You*, damn it!'

'You sound as if you can't wait to get rid of me,' she said tightly, feeling her anger flare.

Dejectedly, he rested his head in his hands and at once she was contrite, remembering Leila's warning. Maybe she had already said too much. Impulsively, she went down on her knees beside his chair and stroked her hand along his forearm. Her nerves, dulled by the shock of her encounter with Bert Halstead, came to vibrant life at the contact and a thrill coursed through her. At once she withdrew her hand as if stung. Their old chemistry still affected her, but she didn't want Kirk to see how strongly in case he thought it was just another ploy to deceive him.

He looked down at the hand she now held primly in her lap. 'Why did you stop?' he asked absently.

'As you keep reminding me, I have no right to touch you,' she said coldly.

'No, you haven't, have you?' he asked, and there was an unmistakable note of challenge in his voice.

Confused, she stood up and went over to her drinks cabinet. 'Would you like a drink?' she asked. 'There isn't much choice, I'm afraid.'

'Scotch will do if you have it,' he suggested.

Thankful for the distraction, she splashed a generous measure into a glass. The bottle had been given to her a couple of Christmases ago and since she never drank Scotch, it was still almost full. Shakily, she poured a brandy for herself and dropped ice cubes into the glasses, then handed Kirk his drink.

He nodded his thanks, but set the glass down on the table beside him without touching the drink. She cradled her own drink in her two hands and curled up in the chair opposite him. He leaned towards her. 'Erin, there's something I want to talk to you about. My God, you're shaking like a leaf!'

At once, he took the drink from her and set it aside, then swept her up into his arms, where she lay like a child against him, cuddling closer to try to still the trembling which racked her body.

'It's just reaction,' he assured her. 'You had a bad fright this evening.'

'B-but I f-feel such a f-fool,' she faltered. She didn't add that this was not only because she couldn't stop shaking, but also because she felt so helpless lying there in his arms, and at the same time so wonderfully comforted by his presence. There was only the thin shield of the bathrobe separating her from his warmth which soon penetrated the fabric, making her feel cosy and reassured. Unconsciously, her arms crept up around his neck and she snuggled closer.

'Better?' he asked.

'Mmm,' she murmured dreamily. 'I've stopped shaking, anyway.'

'I told you it was just the shock. The best thing for you right now is rest.'

Before she could protest, he carried her to the bed and placed her gently on to it, then reached for the fastening of her robe. At once she pulled away, and he frowned impatiently.

'Don't be a fool, I'm only trying to help you.'

'But I haven't got anything on underneath,' she protested.

He shrugged, but his expression was not entirely indifferent. 'So? You didn't mind me seeing you like that before.'

She turned her head away. 'That was different.' Then, their chemistry had been powerfully at work between them, bringing them to at least a semblance of the closeness they had once shared. This time, his concern was purely clinical. And anyway, he now believed she had tried to blackmail Leila. He might be able to act as if that scene had never taken place, but she couldn't. The disgust in his voice and his cruel dismissal of her had wounded her deeply. She realised he was still standing at her bedside, waiting for her response.

'I can undress myself, thank you,' she said primly.

Kirk laughed hollowly. 'Suit youself. If it will satisfy your suddenly acquired sense of decorum, I'll finish my drink—with my back turned. All right?'

Erin didn't respond, so he shrugged again and went to the living room half of the bed-sitter where, true to his word, he picked up his drink and ostentatiously carried it out to the balcony so that his back was turned to her as she stood up and turned the bedclothes down.

The broad set of his back mocked her as she slipped quickly out of the robe and slid between the sheets, then pulled the covers right up under her chin. 'It's all right, you can come back now.'

Taking his time, he strolled back into the room, still holding his drink in one hand. He raised it to her in a mocking salute, then drained it and set the empty glass down on a side table. Then he settled himself into the chair in one corner of her bedroom as if he had every intention of staying.

'What are you doing?' Erin asked nervously.

'Making myself comfortable.'

'I can see that, but I'm in bed now. You've done your duty, so you can leave.'

He remained unperturbed. 'I've only done part of my duty. Once you're safely asleep, I shall tiptoe out of here with a much easier mind.'

There was no way she could fall asleep while he was watching her like this. His steady gaze started her pulses racing and she felt herself flushing with embarrassment at what she was thinking. 'It's no good,' she said crossly. 'I can't possibly sleep with you sitting here like this.'

'Why not?' he asked mildly.

'You know perfectly well why not!' she shot back in exasperation.

'If you mean because I turn you on, I know that. You've already demonstrated it amply enough.'

'Then why don't you go away and leave me alone?' she pleaded.

Kirk looked thoughtful. 'Because you turn me on, too,' he said quietly. 'Haven't you wondered why I was looking for you after you left Eaglewood?'

'To make sure I don't cause you any more trouble?' she volunteered tiredly.

He got up and came over to the bed where he stood looking down at her. 'Nothing that simple,' he confessed. With a sigh, he settled himself on the edge of the bed and took hold of the hand she had left on top of the covers. 'I have to know the truth about you and me.'

'You already have Leila's version,' she said bitterly.

'I said I want the truth. You turn me on, I admit that. But until now I assumed that's all it was—a sexual attraction which I could resist if I wanted to. Except I found I didn't want to, and that bothers me. Why should I feel like this when I'm married to someone else? Every instinct tells me it's wrong to feel like this. I've tried to fight it ever since you came into my life, but, damn it, I can't make the feeling go away.'

'Or me,' Erin added.

'Or you,' he agreed. 'God knows, I've tried, and I'm sure Leila has, too. We've insulted you, belittled you, tried to buy you off—yet you keep turning up like the proverbial bad penny.'

'It could be because I'm the persistent type,' she said.

'I thought of that, but somehow I don't think it's the reason. The trouble is, the only other explanation which makes any sense is that you're telling the truth.'

Forgetting her nakedness, Erin sat bolt upright in the bed, oblivious of the bedclothes which fell away as she did so, exposing her full, round breasts. 'Oh, Kirk, do you really mean that?' she asked, tears of hope gathering in her eyes.

He drew a quick breath at the sight of her, then suddenly she was crushed against him, all the breath driven from her body by the strength of his embrace. His lips found hers and devoured them hungrily, then travelled to the cleft of her breasts where he left a trail of kisses across the white flesh. Involuntarily, she arched her back so that her body was thrust against him, then she gasped as his questing mouth found her nipples and kissed them alternately.

At once she forgot her resolution not to let her affect him in this way and surrendered herself utterly to the joy of being in his arms and the object of his kisses once more. 'Oh, Kirk, I love you,' she said joyfully.

'No!' His cry was that of a man torn between duty and desire, and he wrenched himself away from her to stand a few feet from the bed, looking at her in horror. 'It can't be like this, not yet. Can't you understand?'

Stunned, she sank back against the pillows and groped for the blanket to cover herself, feeling cheap under his horrified gaze. 'What's wrong?' she asked tearfully.

'Like it or not, I have to accept that I'm a married man, until I have evidence to the contrary,' he said flatly. 'That's what I really came here to talk to you about. I didn't mean to let things get out of hand like this.'

The swift transition from passion to coolness had left her shaken and it took her a few minutes to marshal her whirling thoughts. At least he wasn't accusing her of trying to seduce him this time, and he had admitted that the attraction wasn't all one-sided. Nevertheless, the promise of fulfilment so completely made then snatched away just when she had reached a peak of arousal, had left her feeling bruised and aching, as if she had been beaten. Something in his expression must have told him how she felt, because he sat down on the edge of the bed again and took her hand.

'I'm really sorry about this, Erin. I swear I didn't mean it to happen. You just carry me along on a tide. With Leila, I never . . .'

He tailed off as if realising he might say more than he intended. Had he started to say that with Leila he was never carried to the same heights of passion when they made love, as he was with Erin? She hugged the possibility to herself like a guilty secret. While her mind protested at any thought of Kirk and Leila together, it might be easier to accept if she knew it was a purely physical thing, to satisfy Kirk's needs as a man and not, please God, because he found pleasure in Leila's lovemaking.

'What did you want to talk to me about?' she asked, keeping her tone offhand with an effort.

'About us,' he rejoined. 'About where we go from here.'

'I'm listening.'

He regarded her steadily for a moment. In the dressing table mirror she could see her reflection and was disturbed by how childlike and vulnerable she looked, hunched in the roomy bed with the blankets drawn up defensively under her chin. At last he gave an impatient sigh. 'It's no good, you know. With you lying there like that, I can only think of one thing.'

'In that case, perhaps I'd better get up and get dressed,' Erin suggested, guessing the direction of his thoughts. She was having equal difficulty ignoring the stirrings in her own body, aroused as she was by his kisses.

'Do you feel well enough?' he asked.

'The shaking has passed off now, thank goodness. I'll be all right.'

'Well enough to let me take you out to dinner?' he queried.

Although she had had very little to eat since lunchtime at the office, she wasn't very hungry after her experiences with Halstead, but perhaps it would be best if she allowed Kirk to take her to a restaurant. At least there, among a crowd of people, they would be on neutral territory and could talk without the physical distractions which were inevitable here. 'All right,' she agreed. 'Just give me a few minutes while I get dressed.'

Once again he retreated to the balcony and stood looking moodily out towards the rolling surf, while she slipped out of bed and dressed again.

He whistled appreciatively when she appeared beside him a short time later, dressed in a sleeveless knitted dress in a becoming jade colour. Around her waist she had fastened a metallic belt whose links were designed in the shape of conch shells. Although the belt looked expensive, she had been lucky to find it at a handicraft market, and knew it complemented the dress perfectly.

'That was a quick change,' Kirk commented as he escorted her down to where his car was parked. His observation made her wonder if Leila was one of those women who took hours perfecting her appearance and made a habit of arriving late at parties in order to make a grand entrance. It was a fairly safe bet that the heiress didn't know Kirk had come to see Erin, otherwise she would have found some way to keep them apart. Perhaps the other woman thought Erin would be fully occupied with Bert Halstead.

The thought of Bert Halstead made her shiver, and at once Kirk noticed the reaction. 'Cold? I can turn on the car heating if you like.'

'No, I'm fine,' she assured him forcing a smile. 'Someone just walked over my grave, I guess.'

In silence, they continued the drive back towards the city centre, and Erin became curious as to where Kirk was taking her. From the direction in which he was heading, they weren't going to Marcel's. She hoped he would choose somewhere quiet and secluded. Her nerves were frayed enough after tonight's events, and she wanted to hear whatever Kirk had to tell her without interruption. Perhaps they should have stayed at her flat after all. Then she recalled how close they had come to making love then and there and her nerve endings throbbed at the memory. But much as she longed for his caresses, they weren't going to solve anything that way. She also knew that it was not enough for Kirk to belong to her physically. She needed much more from him if there was to be a chance for their marriage in future. Only when he remembered her with his mind as well as his body could they have any sort of future together.

She glanced at him covertly as they drove, revelling in the masterful way he controlled the powerful car with his hands resting lightly on the steering wheel as if he drove by willpower alone. His eyes scanned the road ahead with easy confidence which suggested that he could handle anything.

If only she was half as self-assured, she thought, wishing she could see the path ahead of her clearly enough to steer her life with as much assurance as he steered the car. Instead, her view of the future was clouded by a veil of mist and looming darkly out of it was the fear that she could harm Kirk by saying the wrong thing. Her mouth felt dry and she swallowed convulsively. She shouldn't have agreed to come. What if her very presence was enough to push him to the brink of his endurance?

Looking at him beside her, it was hard to believe Leila could possibly be right, that his peace of mind could be so easily destroyed. Yet she had the evidence of her own eyes. Hadn't she seen what the struggle to remember could do to him when she played the Grieg record at her flat? She would never forget the torment he had endured then. Yet here she was, risking a recurrence because she was too selfishly concerned about her own future, to send him away.

'Take me home,' she said suddenly.

Kirk looked at her in astonishment. 'What? You aren't feeling ill again, are you?'

'No, I'm not ill. I just changed my mind. I don't want to have dinner with you after all, I want you to take me home.'

'The hell I will!' he muttered through clenched teeth. 'This is a sudden change of heart, isn't it?'

'I've told you, I changed my mind. Isn't that supposed to be a woman's prerogative?'

'Maybe. But you and I have too many things that need straightening out between us to play that kind of game. I'm not letting you get away until we have our talk, if I have to tie you to the chair in the restaurant!'

The picture of herself bound to a chair at his table was so extraordinary, she had to fight an urge to laugh. Recognising the beginnings of hysteria, she took a firm grip on her runaway emotions. 'Maybe you won't be so sure of yourself once you hear what I have to tell you.'

At once, he brought the car to a screeching halt at the side of the road, provoking a chorus of angry car horns from the drivers behind them. With an impatient movement, he switched off the engine and swivelled towards her. 'What did you mean by that last remark?'

With a conviction which she was far from feeling, Erin affected a cynical laugh. 'I just felt I couldn't accept any more of your hospitality without coming clean. I'm a fraud—another statistic for your file.'

'So you're saying you made up all this business about being my wife?' he demanded.

Thankful for the darkness in the car which hid her mortified expression from him, she said, 'That's right. I never saw you before the day we met on the assembly line at your factory.'

To her surprise he merely returned to his side of the car and started the engine. When they were cruising along the highway once more, he laughed throatily. 'So you're a fraud, are you? That's interesting.'

Interesting? How could he take it so calmly? She had just confirmed his worst fears about her. It was almost as if he had been expecting her confession and was *pleased* about it. Which didn't make sense, she told herself dizzily. He should have been furiously angry with her and quite happy to accommodate her request to be taken home. Instead, he was continuing the journey as if she hadn't spoken.

A few minutes later he pulled up outside a stately Victorian mansion which looked as if it had occupied the site for a great many years. Mindful of Kirk's threat to tie her to the chair, which past experience of his determination warned her he was quite capable of doing, Erin followed him meekly out of the car park, through floodlit formal gardens and into a room which resembled a Victorian drawing room. Velvet-covered antique settees lined the walls and the romantic strains of a string quartet issued from the main part of the restaurant to which the part they were in formed an anteroom.

Still bewildered by Kirk's strange reaction to her 'confession', Erin allowed herself to be steered to one of the settees. When they were seated, a waiter presented them with a selection of drinks on a silver salver, and a plate of honey-glazed chicken wings as an appetiser.

'Like it?' Kirk asked her as she toyed with her cocktail, having refused to sample the chicken.

'It's very pleasant,' she conceded, at the same time marvelling that he could make polite conversation as if they were an ordinary couple on a perfectly ordinary night out. Maybe Leila was right and his mind had been more affected by his accident than Erin allowed for. It would explain why he hadn't reacted more strongly to her admission that she was a fraud. But if his mind had been damaged, surely he couldn't continue to run a business so capably? Just then a waiter arrived to tell them their table was ready, preventing her from indulging in any further speculation.

The main room was softly lit with candles on each table. The high quality of the napery, cutlery and glassware confirmed her first impression of quiet elegance and luxury. They were shown to a table set in a curtained alcove where they were assured of privacy but could still enjoy the string quartet's gentle chamber music.

Only when they were seated again, ostensibly studying the elaborate menu, did Erin's doubts return. 'Kirk . . .' she began hesitantly.

'I recommend the Oeufs Orléanaise,' he interrupted smoothly. 'It's a superb dish of baked egg on a bed of creamed endive and fresh sage, topped with cream.'

'Yes, whatever you like,' she agreed impatiently. 'I'm not really very hungry.'

He raised a sardonic eyebrow. 'No wonder you got the shakes tonight! I've seen what you bring for lunch at the office and if that's all you've eaten all day, your reaction was probably brought on as much by hunger as anything else!'

With a sigh, she acquiesced and allowed him to order for both of them. She knew Kirk's streak of stubbornness well enough to be sure that they wouldn't do any talking until he was ready, so she might as well accept it with good grace.

To her surprise, the food was so fragrant and artfully presented that it aroused the appetite she thought she had lost. The baked eggs were, indeed, exceptional, as was the main course Kirk chose— smoked salmon encased in crispy filo pastry and served with a delicious hollandaise sauce. Despite her protests that she had eaten too much already, he gestured for the sweets trolley to be brought over and she was faced with a beguiling choice which soon overcame her initial resistance. In the end, she chose a Pêche Cardinal, a tasty confection of firm ripe peaches in a raspberry sauce.

'That's the girl,' Kirk encouraged her. 'I'm glad to see you're finally eating a worthwhile meal.'

'Only because you won't give me any peace until I do,' she retorted. 'I feel like a fish being played on a line.'

'And I'm the fisherman, I suppose?' When she nodded defiantly, he went on, 'I didn't want you collapsing on me again when I tell you what I've got in mind.' Erin waited with barely concealed impatience while he toyed with a fork. When she had decided she could stand the suspense no longer, he looked up. 'I told you I wanted to know the truth about you and me.'

'But I've already told you . . .' she tried.

'I know. You made the whole thing up. A few weeks ago I might have accepted that, but not now. Too much has happened which can't be explained away that simply.'

The pulse in Erin's neck began to jump erratically. This was one possibility Leila hadn't foreseen, that Kirk would want to investigate Erin's story for himself. The heiress had been too sure of herself and her family's influence. She had overlooked or chosen to ignore the fact that Kirk was not one of the Coventry puppets, to be easily manipulated. 'What will you do now?' she asked unhappily.

He regarded her steadily. 'I want you to come away with me for a few days. I need to be alone with you for a while, away from the Corporation.'

And away from Leila? Erin wondered. Aloud, she said, 'Won't there be talk?'

He misunderstood her concern. 'Naturally, I wouldn't want to expose you to any gossip,' he said at once. 'As it happens, I have a perfectly legitimate reason for going away—and taking you with me. The Corporation is interested in some land in the Hastings Valley outside Port Macquarie, for possible future expansion. I was planning to go up and look at it anyway before the merger date, so I may as well go right away. Since my secretary will have to stay behind and run the office in my absence, it's quite in order for me to request a secretary from the pool, to accompany me.'

He waited, obviously expecting some comment from Erin. 'You've thought it all out, haven't you?' she asked tensely.

The note of tension in her voice made him frown.

'From the point of view of what others might think, yes, I have,' he countered. 'But not in the way I think you're suggesting. I'm not planning a dirty weekend, if that's what you're worried about.'

'No, I . . . I didn't think that,' she said hastily. She couldn't very well tell him that her nervousness was on his account, not for herself. He wanted them to go away together to see if it could help him regain his memory. But according to Leila's warning, such an attempt could trigger a complete mental breakdown. If she refused to go, it wouldn't necessarily stop him from trying to remember, so what was she to do? It seemed her only option was to agree to go with him but make sure she did nothing which might provoke another attack of pain. It would confirm her as a fraud in his eyes, she realised miserably, but at least it would protect him. It was all she could think of. 'Very well, I'll go,' she said in a low voice, 'but I'm sure it won't do any good.'

'We'll see soon enough,' he told her. Then he startled her by passing a hand over his eyes.

'What is it? Are you in pain?' she asked worriedly.

He smiled at her, but his voice was strained. 'Over-tiredness, I expect. The merger has entailed a lot of extra work, most of it falling on my shoulders. A few days away from the office will do me a world of good.'

Or a world of harm, Erin thought despondently. He might blame his tiredness on overwork, but she felt sure it was caused by the strain of their talk tonight. Going away with him was bound to make things even worse, but she couldn't see any way out of it. She had never felt so helpless before, even when Kirk was missing. At least then she had hope and faith to sustain her. Now, she had only the knowledge that his apparently robust health was more illusory than even he knew, and she had the power to preserve or destroy it.

The next few days crawled past at a snail's pace as Erin went through the motions of working, always with the prospect of the trip to Port Macquarie weighing heavily on her mind. She should have been over the moon with joy at the idea of a few days away with him, but she couldn't help thinking of the risk involved for him. Try as she might, she couldn't think of any way to get out of going.

The night before they were due to leave, she started to pack with a heavy heart. Because she was barely concentrating on the task the suitcase was half filled before she realised she had automatically packed the clothes Kirk was most likely to remember.

The gypsy skirt and blouse, repaired after the encounter with Bert Halstead, lay on top. The shirt-dress and a bikini which had been part of her trousseau were also neatly packed. During her search for Kirk she had taken these clothes with her, hoping they would provide a visual link for him with their shared past. She had packed them without thinking, and she stared at them in indecision. So far, he hadn't responded to any of the outfits she had chosen, so it seemed unlikely that any harm could come of taking the things with her. Resolutely, she closed the suitcase lid and went to bed, where she tossed and turned for hours before falling into a troubled sleep just as dawn was breaking.

The alarm clock rang much too soon, and reluctantly, she swung her legs over the side of the bed. Kirk would be calling for her in an hour and she still felt desperately worried about going with him.

The face that greeted her in the bathroom mirror looked drawn and anxious and there were mauve shadows under her eyes. She made a wry face at her reflection and swung the cabinet door out at an angle so she wouldn't have to keep looking at herself while she got ready.

Her limbs seemed to be made of lead as her reluctance to go made everything much more of an effort. Less than fifteen minutes remained before Kirk was due to pick her up, when she reached a decision. She couldn't go with him and risk causing a mental breakdown. Somehow she had to get out of the trip—but how?

The doorbell pealed, startling her, and all at once she knew what she was going to do. A flying leap took her back into bed, where she pulled the covers quickly up over her travel clothes. Then she raked her fingers through her hair to tousle it and called feebly, 'Come in!'

Fortunately, she had taken the chain off the door earlier, so she didn't have to get up again to admit Kirk and he came in at once. His eyebrows rose when he caught sight of her in the bed. 'I did say eight o'clock, didn't I?'

Erin sighed pathetically. 'I know, but I seem to have caught one of those twenty-four-hour viruses or something.'

He rested a hand on her forehead, which was hot from her rushing around. This had also lent a feverish flush to her cheeks. 'Mmm, you do seem a bit hot.'

She coughed for effect. 'I feel rather feverish. I'm sorry about the trip.'

From the grim-faced way he looked at her she couldn't tell whether he was annoyed that she had thwarted his plans, or worried about her health. If only she could tell him it was *his* health which had prompted her to deceive him like this!

At last he seemed satisfied. 'It is a shame,' he agreed, 'but I'll have to make the best of it, won't I?'

She nodded and almost wept with relief when he muttered a goodbye and headed for her front door. A moment later she heard the front door slam. Her ruse had worked! Now there was no chance that she could say or do something to cause him pain. But even as she congratulated herself on achieving her aim, she was assailed by depression. She had just thrown away her last chance to be with him before he went out of her life for ever.

Impatiently, she threw back the covers and stood up, automatically smoothing the creases out of her clothes. Then she froze as a sound came from the tiny front hallway. She wasn't alone. She whirled around to find Kirk leaning nonchalantly against the door frame. His arms were folded across his chest and his eyes twinkled with amusement. 'I've heard of rest being the best cure—but five minutes must be some sort of record!'

'I . . . I thought you'd gone,' she stammered.

'So I gather. I had a feeling your illness was a bit sudden, so I stayed around to find out.'

'Why won't you just go away? I told you there's nothing between us and never was.'

'Methinks the lady doth protest too much,' he quoted. 'Now are you finished playing games, or do I have to carry you down to the car?'

'That won't be necessary,' she said coldly. If he expected some sort of apology for her behaviour, he was going to be disappointed.

'Pity,' he murmured, 'I would have enjoyed the exercise.'

'I'm sure you would, since you obviously like pushing people around,' she rejoined angrily. He wasn't to know that her anger was directed wholly at herself for not managing things better. Now she had no choice but to go with him.

For a fleeting moment she was tempted to tell him the real reason for her reluctance but it would do no good. If he believed her at all, he would still take the risk. Apparently neither Leila nor his doctors had told him the full extent of the danger he faced in delving into his past, but even if he knew, he would pay it no more heed than he had ever done to personal danger.

Choking back a sob of frustration, Erin handed him her suitcase and followed him down to the car.

CHAPTER TEN

THE sense of foreboding stayed with Erin throughout the drive to the airport, where she expected that they would board a commercial flight to Port Macquarie. Knowing that they were returning to the same area where Kirk's plane had come down three years ago added to her trepidation. The location of the land the Coventry Corporation planned to buy had seemed like another ill omen when Kirk told her about it. She glanced at him sidelong. Apparently in his present state of mind, the place meant nothing to him— except, of course, as the location of his supposed honeymoon with Leila.

Erin shivered. If they hadn't been driving so fast she would have been tempted to jump out of the car then and there. But it was too late, Kirk was already steering the car into the airport parking lot.

To her surprise, they didn't board a commerical plane at all. Instead they headed for a sleek executive jet which bore the insignia 'C.C.' in a streak of silver along the side.

'The company plane,' Kirk explained in answer to her questioning glance.

'Are you taking us up?' she asked without thinking.

He grinned. 'That'll be the day! No, Bill Charleton, the company pilot, is our chauffeur. What makes you think I can fly a plane?'

She bit her lip and said nothing. Apparently the shock of his accident had also wiped out all recollection of his flying skills. That made two loves he didn't remember, she thought soberly.

The plane's swept-back wings and rear-mounted

turbo engines made it look more like a scaled-down jumbo jet than a private plane, she thought. In normal circumstances, Kirk would have been unable to resist giving her a detailed rundown of its features and flight capabilities. He would have been able to estimate how many nautical miles it was capable of flying without refuelling, its maximum airspeed and a hundred other details. But these were not normal circumstances, she was reminded when he showed no further interest in the plane.

As they settled themselves into the spacious cabin, she pondered anew on the problem of how she was going to keep Kirk from using her to probe into his past, perhaps with disastrous consequences. She had been so angry with him for his high-handed treatment this morning that she hadn't said a word to him on the way to the airport. Maybe that was the solution. If she could only keep up the pretence of being annoyed, it might provide an effective barrier between them.

Staying angry at him was easier said than done, she discovered as she watched him clip his seatbelt into place with capable hands. Unlike normal planes, this one had armchair seating arranged around a coffee table and Kirk was able to stretch his long legs out in front of him. He hooked one ankle over the other in a pose which was so characteristic that it brought a lump to Erin's throat. She forced herself to conjure up a mental picture of him in bed with Leila, their bodies entwined. At once, her anger returned in full force and the glowering look she directed at him across the plane was filled with genuine fury, but against Leila, not Kirk who was only acting as he thought to be right.

'You're not still angry because I forced you to come on this trip?' he asked, intercepting the look.

'What do you think?' she retorted.

'It won't get us anywhere if you insist on behaving like an iceberg,' he said mildly.

Which was precisely her aim, she thought grimly. The only question was—how long could she keep this act up?

Her task was made easier by the fact that once they were airborne, Kirk promptly closed his eyes and went to sleep. Erin must have dozed off, too, worn out after a succession of sleepless nights caused by the prospect of this trip, because the next thing she knew, there was a series of jolts and the screech of tyre rubber on tarmac.

'Are we here already?' she asked, slightly disorientated. Hardly more than a few minutes seemed to have passed since they had taken off from Sydney.

'It isn't a very long flight,' Kirk reminded her, unfastening his seatbelt. When he reached across to unclip hers, the warmth of his touch seared the back of her hand like a brand. She jumped slightly and he frowned. 'Must you always react as if I bite when I touch you?'

She must remember to stay angry, she told herself. 'Maybe you shouldn't touch me, then,' she suggested coldly.

He sighed. 'I thought that was the whole point of us being here.'

'My, my, and all the time I thought it was to look at land for your precious Corporation!' she mocked.

With an indrawn breath of annoyance, he stood up. 'You're being deliberately difficult,' he snapped. 'What's got into you, Erin? Don't you want to help me any more?'

'The only person I want to help is myself,' she said, hating herself for hurting him like this. 'Remember, I admitted that I was a fraud. You were the one who didn't want to accept it. Maybe you will after this trip.'

Without a word, he turned and stalked out of the plane, not even pausing to lend her a hand down the stairway. Watching him stride towards the terminal building, Erin couldn't remember when she had felt so utterly miserable. Why couldn't he have accepted her 'confession' in Sydney instead of dragging the situation out like this? At least that would have been a clean break. It was like slow torture being with him like this, unable to show her real feelings for fear of causing him irreparable harm.

Because the land they were to look at was at Wauchope, some distance out of Port Macquarie, Kirk had reserved rooms for them at a hotel south of the town, in what he had described earlier as rain-forest country. A rented car awaited them at the airport and as soon as Kirk had stowed their luggage on board, they drove the short distance to their hotel. He maintained an icy silence throughout the whole operation, and Erin felt the tension growing inside her like a knot. She had deliberately provoked him and now she was paying the consequences, but at what cost to herself? When Kirk went to America after this, he would remember her with loathing, while her last memory of him would be the anger which now lay between them like a tangible thing.

At any other time, Erin would have been delighted by their rooms, which were on the second floor of a refurbished sandstone building which dated back to the days of convict settlement. Each room opened on to a planked wooden verandah and across the road was a stand of lush, prehistoric rain forest, giving her an idea of how the whole area must once have looked. The forest gave the area a dark, brooding atmosphere which was so in keeping with her mood that Erin felt like laughing hysterically, except that she would break the gloomy spell. But by now, Kirk was so thoroughly annoyed with her that she doubted whether it would have made any difference.

After a lunch eaten mostly in silence at the hotel,

they set off for Wauchope, where Kirk had an appointment with a local real estate agent who was to show them the parcel of land. The agent, Mac Healey, turned out to be a veritable ray of sunshine in contrast to Kirk and Erin. If he noticed the tension between Kirk and his 'secretary', he said nothing but made a determined effort to cheer everyone up.

'If Coventry moves in here, you'll never regret it,' he enthused. 'I've been saying for years that the mineral potential in this area hasn't been exploited beyond a fraction of its potential.'

'What sort of minerals do you find here?' Erin asked politely, since Kirk didn't seem inclined to break his stony silence.

Mac flashed her a grateful smile. 'They've found copper, tin, manganese—you name it, even gold,' he explained. 'Mainly though, this area is known for its timber—cedar in the colonial days, and blackbutt today. Then we have beef cattle, pigs and mixed farming.'

'You forgot to mention the bees,' Kirk intervened dryly.

Mac shot him a startled look, not sure whether Kirk was joking or not and anxious not to offend a potentially valuable client. 'Er—yes, we have bee-keeping, too.' With obvious relief, he indicated the turn-off which led to the land in which Coventry was interested and Kirk swung the car off the main road on to a gravel side road. Mac Healey had volunteered to drive but had also been rebuffed curtly by Kirk on that point.

Erin felt sorry for the agent. The situation between her and Kirk was nothing to do with him, and yet he was getting the brunt of it in cold silences and unprovoked jibes from Kirk. 'Surely Coventry wouldn't put a factory out *here*?' she said in an attempt to divert Kirk's attention from the hapless agent.

'In the first place, it would no longer qualify for the description 'out here' if Coventry moved in,' said Kirk with exaggerated patience. 'The workers and the amenities for them would naturally follow. However, although the Corporation is negotiating a decentralisation package with the Government, the immediate value of the land lies in its timber.'

Suitably chastened, Erin sat back in her seat and exchanged a sympathetic smile with the estate agent. 'Seems I'm not the only target today,' his look clearly told her.

After that Erin concentrated on playing her role of dutiful secretary, aware that her performance earned her frequent scathing looks from Kirk. But she was careful to maintain the barrier of tension between them. She knew he was hurt and puzzled by the change in her behaviour since they left Sydney, but there was no way she could explain her actions to him without revealing Leila's warning and her own anxiety about his health.

By the time they left Wauchope later that afternoon, she was emotionally and physically exhausted. She hadn't dreamed that staying angry could be so draining. Only by constantly reinforcing her mental vision of Kirk and Leila together could she maintain her feelings of antagonism, and her nerves were ragged with the strain. They dropped Mac Healey off at the office of another client in Port Macquarie, and Erin heaved a sigh of relief. At least alone with Kirk, she could drop the pretence of being a dutiful employee.

To her surprise, instead of heading out of town back towards the hotel, Kirk took a different turning which led towards the beach. At once Erin tensed, thinking of the last time she had come this way. Then she had been accompanied by a policeman and had been faced with the very real possibility that she would soon have to identify her husband's body. However, the plane had been empty and Erin had had to cope with the daunting discovery that Kirk had disappeared without trace.

'Where are we going?' she asked apprehensively.

'What's the matter? Don't you like driving along the beach?' he taunted.

'Not along this particular beach,' she told herself, involuntarily picturing it as she had last seen it. Then it had been cordoned off and crawling with police skindivers and detectives, as well as press photographers and the inevitable sightseers. Aloud, she said. 'Not with you.'

'I see—still playing hard to get,' he teased, but there was a hard edge of annoyance in his voice.

'I'm not playing at anything,' she flared. 'I just think that this has gone far enough.'

'You should have thought of that before you started it,' Kirk rejoined. 'You might play games, but it's time you learned that I don't.'

Dear God, what did he have in mind? For the first time it occurred to her that he might have planned this trip as a way of punishing her. Maybe he had never really believed her all along, but had only pretended to soften in order to get her to come here with him. Her fear must have shown on her face, because his expression relaxed slightly. 'Don't look so scared, I told you I didn't come here for a dirty weekend. I wanted to get to the bottom of this mystery, and I intend to if it's the last thing I do.'

The last thing . . . the phrase triggered a warning in Erin's tired brain. What was she thinking of, allowing him to provoke her like this? He might not know what a risk he was taking with his stubborn insistence on delving into his past, but she did—and she was not going to be the instrument of his destruction.

'Suit yourself,' she said, keeping her tone light, 'but no matter how much you try to push me you won't get any more answers than the one I've already given you.' She gave him a moment to digest her comment, then asked with deliberate detachment, 'Where *are* we going, by the way?'.

'To Leila's beach house,' he said grimly. At her startled look, he went on, 'But don't worry—I only have to collect some files she inadvertently left there on her last visit.' Unconsciously, Erin had slumped in her seat and let out a sigh of relief so that he looked at her in disgust. 'You really do have a one-track mind, don't you?' he said distastefully.

He brought the car to a halt outside an imposing double-storeyed building. Erin had been expecting a modest cottage, certainly not this impressive white stone villa. It nestled possessively against the hillside and was shaded by a lush native garden leading all the way down to the beach with the sea beyond.

No wonder Leila had been able to carry out her deception so successfully! With the beach literally at her feet she would have been able to take Kirk inside and nurse him back to health without anyone knowing he was there. Since there were no other neighbours for a considerable distance on each side, Leila's privacy was assured.

'Are you coming inside?' Kirk asked as he started to get out of the car.

At the thought of Leila's deception, conceived and carried out in this very house, Erin felt a surge of revulsion. 'No, I'll wait here.'

He shrugged. 'As you like, but I wouldn't stay inside the car if I were you. You'll cook without the air-conditioner running.'

Resignedly, Erin got out of the car and leaned against it, staring pensively out to sea. The sight of the mighty South Pacific Ocean rolling aggressively against the coastline calmed and soothed her, and she welcomed the caress of the sea breeze against her hot cheeks. So that the breeze could cool the inside of the car, she opened the front doors wide, then glanced back towards the house to see if there was any sign of Kirk yet. The house made her feel uneasy, and she would be glad to get away.

The sound of voices coming from inside the house startled her. She hadn't expected anyone to be here. The other voice was a woman's, so perhaps Leila employed a housekeeper to look after the place in her absence.

Erin frowned as the sound of the exchange became angrier, and automatically she started towards the house. Close to where she stood, a picture window opened on to a small wooden patio, and she stepped on to it, feeling guilty at the realisation that she was going to eavesdrop. She told herself the day was drawing near when Kirk would leave for America, so every minute with him was precious and she needed every scrap of information about him to remember later, when he was gone.

The voice that reached Erin's ears certainly didn't belong to any housekeeper. 'How could you waste your time with that cheap little blackmailer?'

'Leila, listen to me, I've already told you . . .'

Erin froze in horror. The voice was Leila's! Kirk must have known she would be here, which explained why he was so anxious to detour here instead of returning to the hotel. What was he trying to do?

Much nearer to Erin this time, Leila's voice came again. 'I'll show you what she is!' Suddenly the sliding window was pulled aside and Leila stood framed in the opening, staring at Erin as if she had just crawled out from under a rock. Erin quailed beneath the savage scrutiny, but stood her ground.

Leila emerged on to the patio, followed by Kirk. 'See,' she said triumphantly, 'your honourable little secretary is shamelessly listening to everything we've said, and doesn't care who knows it, from the look of her!'

'Were you listening, Erin?' Kirk asked quietly.

Hurt beyond bearing, Erin tossed her head defiantly. 'What if I was? I'm supposed to play by the rules, it seems, but you can do whatever you like!'

'What in hell does that mean?'

'It means I know what you're up to, Don Sands—or should it be Don Juan? What were you planning to do—sleep with us on alternate nights to see how we compare?'

His expression became thunderous. 'Stop it, Erin! If you'd been listening to what I was saying in here, you would know . . .'

'I know enough to know when I'm licked,' she interrupted tearfully. She didn't want to hear what had passed between him and Leila, and she definitely didn't want to hear him say how sorry he was that the trip up here hadn't proved anything. She was sure that was what he was about to say.

There was no way she could fight Leila's ruthless determination, so she turned to the heiress with a heavy heart. 'You've won, if that's what you want to hear. You were right about the difference between you and me. I can't gamble with the life of someone I love. If that's a weakness, I don't want to change, ever!'

Choking on the last words, she stumbled off the patio and back to the car. The keys were still in the ignition and she jumped into the front seat and slammed the door behind her. Blinded by tears, she reached across and jerked the other door shut, then started the engine.

'Erin, wait a minute! Listen . . .'

Whatever else Kirk might have had to say was drowned in the roar of the engine as she slammed the car into gear. With a kangaroo leap, it started forward. In the driving mirror, she caught a last glimpse of

Kirk standing in the cloud of dust churned up by her rapid departure.

A car horn blared nearby and she realised she was weaving all over the road. She didn't care what happened to her any more, but she didn't want to kill or injure an innocent person, so she steered back to her own side of the road and scrubbed at her eyes with the back of her hand until her vision cleared.

She had lost Kirk, that was all her whirling brain could assimilate. Leila had won. And yet Erin had won, too. By distracting Kirk from his reason for bringing her here she had prevented any recurrence of the agonising headaches which could have destroyed his mind. No matter that he still believed he was married to Leila, at least he was well, and without Erin he would be freed from the reminders of his past which might harm him. At all costs she must cling to that. He would have his chance at happiness, even if it was at the cost of her own.

Ahead of her the road narrowed as it wound around a steep rock face. On one side was the wall of multi-hued sandstone and the other side a sheer cliff where the road dropped down to the sand and the sea. She was in no mood to appreciate the splendour of the scenery, however. All she wanted at that moment was to return to the hotel, collect her things and catch the first available flight back to Sydney. She could leave the hire car at the airport for Kirk to attend to when he got there. At least he wasn't stranded. Leila must have driven to the beach house by car, so she would look after him.

At this thought, the tears threatened to brim over again as she steered the car around the corner, keeping well to the centre of the road and away from the crumbling clifftop. There was a roar of sound from the other direction and without warning, a huge semi-trailer came bearing down on her. Instinctively she steered away from it and found herself hurtling towards the sheer drop. There was only time to throw her hands up to protect her face before she felt a sickening jolt and blackness closed in on her.

'Erin—can you hear me?'

She was dead, she had to be. The last thing she remembered was the car hurtling out of control towards the cliff. There was no way she could have avoided going over the edge.

Yet when she forced her eyes open, she found that the car was miraculously wedged against a tree which grew at an angle almost parallel to the road. Its roots tenaciously gripped the meagre soil at the roadside, while its branches hung out over the cliff like Rapunzel's hair. Through the car window, someone was gripping her shoulder tightly. Painfully, she turned her head to see who it was. Oh God, not Kirk! She couldn't take any more of his anger, not now.

Surprisingly, there was no anger at all in his voice. 'Don't move, Erin. We'll have you out of there in a few minutes, but the car is very precariously balanced. Are you listening?'

She had closed her eyes against a wave of dizziness, but opened them again as his tone changed. 'Don't shout. I heard you the first time.'

'I'm sorry, I didn't mean to sound sharp. Tell me, are you hurt anywhere? Can you feel your legs?'

Careful not to upset the balance of the car, she flexed her leg muscles experimentally. 'Everything seems to be working, except that I'm wedged in here.'

'The police rescue squad will have you out of there before you know it,' said Kirk, relief in his voice. 'They're on their way.'

A few minutes later the rescue vehicle arrived with a banshee wail of sirens and Kirk was ushered out of their way. With a last squeeze of her shoulder, he stepped aside. As soon as the paramedics made sure that she wasn't in need of medical attention, the rescue team went to work. They were quick and efficient, but it still seemed like an age before they managed to free the jammed door and lever the steering wheel off her so she could be helped out of the car. As she climbed gingerly out, the tree supporting the vehicle creaked and groaned alarmingly, but it held firm and she reached the roadway in safety.

Only when she looked back at the car did she appreciate how truly miraculous her escape had been, and relief made her legs give way under her. Before she could fall, Kirk swept her up into his arms and carried her back around the corner to where another car was parked on the roadside.

'Yours?' she asked as he placed her on the back seat.

'Leila's,' he explained apologetically. 'I had to come after you, and borrowing her car was the only choice I had, since you'd taken off in mine.'

'What did she say about that?' Erin couldn't help asking.

'I don't know. I didn't stop to ask.' He went down on one knee beside the open car door and took both her hands in one of his large ones. 'Oh, Angel, I thought I'd lost you!'

She must still be groggy from the accident. Surely he hadn't called her Angel? Before she could ask him, an ambulance man came around the corner and leaned into the car.

'We'll take you to the hospital now, miss.'

She couldn't go to a hospital, not now when she had to ask Kirk why he had called her by a pet name he couldn't possibly remember. 'There's no need for the hospital,' she protested. 'I'm all right, really.'

They still insisted on checking her over thoroughly. 'Beats me how you managed it, but you're unhurt,' the ambulance man told her. 'You're a lucky young woman, but you were unconscious for a time after the impact, so there could be a concussion.'

'Will she be all right if I stay with her and watch her?' Kirk queried.

The man nodded reluctantly. 'We can't force her to go to hospital, although it would be advisable in the circumstances. But since she doesn't want to, the next best thing is rest and quiet, and someone will have to check on her every few hours to make sure she's still lucid.'

'I can do all that, and at the first sign of any problems, she'll be at the hospital in record time, I promise.'

Then Erin had to make a statement to the police at the scene, and it took every ounce of willpower she had to quell her rising sense of excitement while she gave them all the details she could remember of the accident. Finally, the police said they had all the information they needed, and the rented car was hooked up to a waiting tow truck, nudged back from the cliff edge and towed away towards Port Macquarie.

Blessed silence closed around them as the last of the cars with their lights and sirens, drove away. Thankfully, Erin sank back against the seat cushions of Kirk's borrowed car. Although she had no serious injuries, her body felt as if it had been used as someone's punching bag. In the morning she would be a mass of bruises where she had collided with the steering wheel when the car came up against the tree, and she ached all over.

A hand lightly brushed the hair back from her temples and she looked up into Kirk's anxious eyes. 'Are you sure you're all right?'

'Apart from a few bruises, I'm fine,' she assured him. Then she remembered what he had said to her earlier and jerked upright, her aches and pains momentarily forgotten. 'What did you call me before the ambulance man interrupted?' she asked, and held her breath as she waited for his reply.

He thought for a moment. 'I think it was Erin . . . or was it 'darling'? Oh—you mean "Angel".'

'Kirk!' she screamed in heartfelt joy. 'You can remember!'

Wordlessly, he nodded, then reached for her and enfolded her tightly in his arms as if he never intended to let her go. With her face buried in his shoulder, Erin began to cry uncontrollably.

At the sound of her sobs, he held her at arm's length and his finger traced the river of tears sliding down her cheeks. 'Hey, what's this for?'

'I'm crying because I'm so h-happy,' she gasped. 'Oh, Kirk, this is so wonderful! When did you regain your memory?'

'When I came around that corner and found you unconscious in a car that looked as if a breath of wind could blow it over the edge. I was terrified for you! Seeing the woman I loved in such danger did something to my mind.'

'But what about the pain?'

'It was pretty bad for a while. I thought I might be going mad with it, but only for a minute or two. I guess I was more worried about you than myself, and that gave me the strength to ride it out. Then, suddenly, the pain was gone. I knew who I was . . . and who you were,' he said, smiling tenderly.

Erin wrinkled her brow in puzzlement. 'Wait a minute. You said the woman you loved was in danger, but that was *before* your memory returned.'

'You little fool,' he said indulgently, 'that's what I was telling Leila at the beach house, and why I asked you whether you'd heard what I said to her. Evidently you didn't, or you wouldn't have taken off like that. When she turned up there and I realised she'd been spying on me, I told her I couldn't go on living with her as her husband, no matter what the truth was between you and me. You see, Don Sands had fallen in love with you, too.'

A thousand questions buzzed in her brain, but Kirk refused to let her talk any more until he had made her comfortable in the back of the car and driven them both back to the hotel, where he overruled her protests and helped her into bed.

Only when she was propped up against the pillows and he was seated on the edge of the bed would he let her ask any of her questions. Even then, he kept interrupting to shower her with tender kisses.

'Stop that!' she protested half-heartedly. The truth was, she didn't ever want him to stop, but there was so much she needed to know about the last three years, before her mind would be completely at rest.

'I know how Leila found you and convinced you she was your wife,' she began, 'and I guessed that her housekeeper, Mrs Niland, must have helped her to carry the deception through. But I don't understand how she was able to produce a marriage certificate and wedding photographs.'

'The certificate was obviously a forgery and the photos were retouched,' he murmured as his lips roved over her throat and shoulders. He straightened up. 'Leila took some snapshots of me while I was recovering. She must have had my face superimposed over some wedding pictures. I was told they were being developed, so I didn't get to see them until I'd been at the beach house for some time. Leila has the money and resources to buy anything she wants—even people.'

'Which was how she prevented anyone who might have recognised you from getting too close,' Erin agreed. 'She told me so after that awful scene at Eaglewood when she accused me of being a blackmailer.'

'That was really her undoing,' Kirk pointed out. Erin's eyes widened with surprise as he explained. 'I still didn't remember you then, but I knew you well enough to be sure you wouldn't stoop to blackmail. Besides, you turned my offer of money down the first time we met in my car.'

'But you called me a . . .'

'I called *Leila* a little bitch,' he corrected. 'I was so angry that I had to get out of the room before I did her some harm.'

So that was why he had walked out. 'I thought you believed her,' Erin admitted. 'She had all the so-called evidence and I had no way of proving who I was.'

His lips brushed the edge of her hairline, carefully skirting a bruise which had begun to darken her forehead. 'You had the strongest evidence of all—the truth.'

'Even when I told you I was a fraud?'

'Especially then. That's when I knew you must love me a hell of a lot, if you were willing to sacrifice yourself for me. But what I don't understand is why you stuck to your story about being a con artist even after I'd given you the benefit of the doubt.'

Shakily, she repeated Leila's dire warning that forcing Kirk to remember his past could provoke an attack of pain strong enough to destroy his mind. 'I was so frightened for you,' she whispered.

Kirk grinned, and at the sight of that boyish smile, so very dear to her, a thrill went through her. 'I only look fragile,' he smiled. 'The headaches were pretty bad, especially just before my memory returned. The doctors said they were brought on by guilt. I guess part of me always knew I was living a lie, so now that conflict is resolved, I shouldn't have any more attacks. Even so, I doubt whether they could have been fatal. That was probably another invention of Leila's.'

Erin combed her hair with one hand. 'She loves you, you know,' she said with an effort.

He shook his head. 'She loves someone she invented, called Don Sands. But she loves the Coventry Corporation far more than any human being.' He began to inspect the bedclothes with rapt attention, not looking at her. 'Angel, there's something I want to explain about my relationship with Leila.'

Erin touched a silencing finger to his lips. 'There's nothing to explain. What happened wasn't your fault.'

'That's just it—nothing happened,' he ground out.

'What are you saying?'

'I'm saying that despite everything, I never slept with Leila Coventry. In the beginning, I was too ill. Then later—well, it just didn't work. The doctors said it was psychological, like the headaches. I can see why now—my subconscious was telling me something was wrong. After a while, Leila moved into another room. But whatever hang-ups I had with her didn't exist with you—as I found out that night I stayed at your flat. So you see, although I couldn't remember that we were married, my subconscious did.'

Erin's heart swelled with joy. He was hers and always had been. 'You didn't have to tell me,' she assured him, but she was glad that he had. Now the last element of uncertainty was gone. 'What will happen to Leila now?' she asked.

It seemed Kirk already knew about the terms of Henry Coventry's will. 'She won't lose her precious Corporation. As far as anybody needs to know, she was married, but her husband ran off with his secretary. I can stand that if you can. I think she'll find that a business is pretty cold comfort in one's old age, and that is probably punishment enough, don't you agree?'

Erin readily gave her assent. The last thing she

wanted was to expose Leila publicly, which would involve them all in the resulting publicity. She and Kirk were together again, that was all Erin cared about. Willingly, she surrendered to his kisses and the fiery warmth of his embrace. His breathing grew quicker and with an oath he stood up, stripped off his clothes and slid into the bed beside her.

The pain of her bruises was forgotten as she gave herself up to the ecstasy of being in his arms once more, with all the barriers finally gone.

'Erin,' he said after a long time, 'Don Sands fell in love with you. How did he compare with Kirk Wilding, in your eyes?'

Her expression became impish. 'I can't say yet. It's been so long since someone called Kirk Wilding made love to me that I have no basis for comparison.'

For answer, he claimed her mouth in a deep, satisfying kiss which sent flames of desire racing along her veins and started her heart pounding so violently she thought it would leap from her chest. Then they were consumed in a fire of passion so intense that all else was forgotten—except each other.

Take these
4 best-selling novels
FREE

Yes! Four sophisticated, contemporary love stories by four world-famous authors of romance FREE, as your introduction to the Harlequin Presents subscription plan. Thrill to **Anne Mather**'s passionate story BORN OUT OF LOVE, set in the Caribbean.... Travel to darkest Africa in **Violet Winspear**'s TIME OF THE TEMPTRESS....Let **Charlotte Lamb** take you to the fascinating world of London's Fleet Street in MAN'S WORLD .... Discover beautiful Greece in **Sally Wentworth**'s moving romance SAY HELLO TO YESTERDAY.

Harlequin Presents...

The very finest in romance fiction

Join the millions of avid Harlequin readers all over the world who delight in the magic of a really exciting novel. EIGHT great NEW titles published EACH MONTH! Each month you will get to know exciting, interesting, true-to-life people . . . . You'll be swept to distant lands you've dreamed of visiting .... Intrigue, adventure, romance, and the destiny of many lives will thrill you through each Harlequin Presents novel.

Get all the latest books before they're sold out!
As a Harlequin subscriber you actually receive your personal copies of the latest Presents novels immediately after they come off the press, so you're sure of getting all 8 each month.

Cancel your subscription whenever you wish!
You don't have to buy any minimum number of books. Whenever you decide to stop your subscription just let us know and we'll cancel all further shipments.